Let's Not & Sleigh We Did

Let's Not & Sleigh We Did

© copyright 2024 J.P. Sterling

Editors: Rebecca Carpenter, Barren Acres Editing

This is a work of fiction. Any mention of names, places, and characters is fiction and for entertainment purposes only.

Not liable for any sudden obsession with fluffy cows.

Contents

Let's Not & Sleigh We Did

Oh, oh, the mistletoe, hung where I did NOT see.

My brother's friend waits for me and gets down on one knee—*What is happening?*

Somebody stop it, please!

Oh, those dreamy blue eyes batting at me, and all the words he dares to say.

This is bad. Like really, really bad.

We're now planning a wedding day.

But it's all for a good reason, not love.

Oh, cough, cough, let's not bust out the L-word.

It's purely business.

It was a solid plan until it wasn't.

So maybe I love him, but we agreed not to do that . . . *whoops!*

Let's Not and Sleigh We Did **is a fake marriage of convenience, brother's best friend, just-kisses-but-all-the-swoons romcom. Oh, yeah, there's a fluffy cow too.**

Introduction

Welcome to the Autumn-perfect, Christmas-perfect, and falling-in-love-perfect town of Mapleton, Vermont. If this is your first trip to town, sit back and prepare for fun banter and shenanigans to bring you all the feels. If you are returning to Mapleton, welcome home.

One

Noelle Winters

"I met someone online, and I think she's *the one,*" Nate, my twin brother states. He's fifteen minutes older than me, but that hasn't translated to wisdom, and Nate has clearly lost more than a couple IQ points to even consider this an option.

"First of all, that sounds like an excellent way to get murdered." I scoot to the edge of my chair, doing my best to not sound like I'm mothering my fully grown adult brother. "How do you even know this person is who they say they are?"

He's smug, silent as he sits across from me at the squeaky dinner table we share every night as roommates. Almost four years ago, we divided an old country farmhouse in Mapleton, Vermont. Not because it was our dream to be roomies.

Quite the contrary.

When we turned eighteen, our dear, sweet-but-ever-so- exhausted parents said, "Go to college or move out."

College was a "meh" for me. I have an overzealous entrepreneurial spirit with an all-consuming dream of working with horses.

Correction.

Not a dream.

An obsession.

An obligation.

Life's purpose.

Since horses can't read, they don't seem to care about my lack of a paper degree or certificate. And, I couldn't have a horse in the city limits of Richmond, so I set my eyes on a more affordable rural town. Nate didn't want anything to do with more school either, so we moved two hours away to Mapleton *together.*

Why together?

Because stuff is *expensive.*

"And," he continues, while rubbing the faintest shadow of blond whisker hair on his baby cheeks, "I'm moving to Florida to be with her—next week."

"Whoa, whoa, whoa." My spine straightens from the bottom like a zipper running along my vertebrae. "Tell me you aren't going to tell me what I think you are going to tell me."

"Sorry, Noelle." His lashes lower, hooding his almond-shaped eyes that twin with mine.

My adrenaline shoots through the ceiling. Nate has lost his marbles.

Nobody just up and moves to another state, where they know nobody, to be with a person who might not even be real—or worse, she might be luring him into a trap—*like a serial killer*. I peer at him just like Mom did when we were kids when he was in trouble. My eyes are wide and, hopefully, my gaze is scary and piercing. "What are you thinking? Florida? You're being completely irrational. You can't just move there."

"I've made my decision." His voice rises into a positive inflection. "I can't go unless I know you'll be okay, and I know you can't afford the place without me. I already thought of everything. I talked to Luke, you know, my friend from high school. He's attending Mapleton's private college, and he'd said he could probably move in. He has to talk to his parents first, since they are paying for his college tuition and board, but it's not going to be an issue."

My brow furrows as I resist the urge to hurl in my lap. Visions of the soggiest kiss I'd ever experienced dance around my head, and my teenage vow to never kiss anyone on a dare again echoes like a loud and annoying police siren.

I was pretty much a hopeless romantic before Luke, but he almost ruined me from kissing *for life*.

I don't take that lightly.

I shudder as I push the painful memory away. "I can't live with Lu—"

"He's not as bad as he used to be!" Nate interrupts, flailing his arms wildly in protest at my refusal, which illustrates even more he's gone insane. "He's the only person I trust to take care of you," Nate rushes. "I'm not sure I can find anyone else who needs a roommate. Plus, all the apartments I've seen for rent are so expensive. You'll never be able to afford this house. Luke's parents are loaded, so he'll have no problem paying."

One of my brows takes a sharp northerly hike as if pointing to one of the things that's always bothered me about Luke, even before we kissed. He's always been a spoiled rich kid. The fact that he's still demanding his parents to pay for his rent clearly shows he never grew out of that stage. "Isn't he a little old to rely on his parents?"

"Not really. He's going to college, and his parents want him to focus on getting his prelaw degree so he can eventually take over his dad's law firm. At least while his parents pay for everything, he's listening to them."

"I remember his parents." My deer-in-the-headlights stare finds the wall. His mother is the epitome of country club chic, always wearing a white tennis skirt and warmup jacket without even a hair out of place. She pencils on a Cindy Crawford mole every morning, like she's done every single day since the 80s. I used to think it was weird, but it's the kind of crazy thing that happens when a lie is allowed to get out of hand. Like, you sold everyone on this mole forty years ago, and it would be pretty weird to finally admit it was all a farce now. It's fine, really. Except for the random times she "sweats" it off, but everybody knows not to say anything about it.

Oh, and Luke's dad always has a joke for everyone, and he never runs out of gum. Every time I see him, he's refreshing his wad with a new stick. It must be some type of ADD stimming. Overall, both his parents are great people. I grimace hard as there isn't even anything to consider for me because there's a massive *but,* I don't care if Luke's parents can pay *all* the rent.

There's no way I'll ever live with Luke Slobberlips.

Cough.

I'll work double shifts at the stable. I'll find a side hustle—or two!

Desperation wraps around me, my brain throwing around all the horrible jobs I will need, but none of them sound as terrible as living with Luke. I'll do anything to make this work.

Sell my kidney on the black market?

I'm not above it. Sharing is caring, right? Save a life.

Nobody is going to make me live with Luke. I walk to the fridge, grab a cold bottle of water, and practically chug it down before I come up for air. "So, yeah." I swallow the distaste in my throat with the last of my water. "You can tell Luke thanks for the offer, but ah, I'm good."

"Are you sure?" He tips his head, as if weighing the good and the bad. "I paid rent through the end of the month, but you only have one week to produce double the rent for next month. Not to mention double utilities, while still making your truck payment."

"I got it. It'll all work out." I breathe deeply, relaxing back into my chair as I nearly avoided a colossal catastrophe. If I had an allergy to anyone, it would be Luke. It's absurd to think I could live with . . .

Ding!

"Oh." I jump up from my chair as the oven timer beeps. "TV dinners are done." I slip on an oven mitt and shimmy both dinner trays out of the oven. All the while my brain is doing math. Nate is about as clueless as guys come, only leaving me about a week's notice to figure this out. Shaking my head, I plop both cardboard trays on the table and grumble, "Dinner is served."

"You know"—Nate takes his napkin, whips it open and places it on his lap— "you might enjoy living with Luke, because the dude can actually cook."

"He can?" I lower myself back onto my chair and stare at my dry rice and cardboard chicken, the same thing I've heated up in the oven every night this week. I pretend to relax in my chair, leaning all the way back to make Nate stop worrying about me. He must stop planning my life because he has horrible ideas. Maybe, he should think more about this serial killer he's about to marry. It's just ridiculous to think I could ever lived with Luke. Relief seeps into my shoulders as I think about this near miss. "Well, I love a man who can cook, but I don't care if he's a master chef. I'd rather eat TV dinners for the rest of eternity than live with Luke."

Oop. There it is again. The dry heaves. It's the sensation I feel when my mind focuses too much on Luke Halo.

Balling my fist, I cover my mouth and swallow the phlegm that crawled up my throat. It must be like a natural antibiotic, or something of the sort, where my body must cleanse the pallet of my aversion to Luke.

The mere memory of his face can send me into anaphylactic shock.

And that can't happen because I now have to work twice as hard to get all these bills paid.

Luke needs to stay out of sight.

Cough.

There's the phlegm again.

There's absolutely no way I can ever live with Luke, and Nate needs to get this idea out of his head. "No," I mumble through my first bite of rice, the staleness of the grain hitting the taste buds so much harder tonight for some reason. "I cannot allow Luke to move in. I would rather move back home with Mom and Dad before I let him move in." I grab my water to wash the seriously sticky, bland mush down, and come back up for air blurting out, "Besides, I can find my own roommate."

Here's the thing, I never asked for a twin. It's not something you have an option to upgrade to in your birth experience, but for the most part, Nate and I have done life together. We don't always agree on everything, but that's what makes the twin things even more special. We are perfectly fine to call each other out because we know each other's thoughts, even better than we know our own sometimes. At this point, my twin power is flashing alarms that Nate is out of his mind! There is no way I will ever take his advice anymore.

"I'm offering you a perfect solution. The rent will be paid, and Luke will be here to help you." Nate throws his hands in the air, mumbling under his breath, "Why do you have to be so stubborn?"

"Have fun living with a serial killer." I tuck my chin to my chest, and I swallow again as the rice is so sticky it needs a double swallow.

Yeah, I'll post an ad for a roommate, and I'll find someone so much better than even Nate.

How hard can that be?

The next day, I wake up early and devour all the Help Wanted ads I can find online. The only things I find require day hours when I'm needed at the stable. I don't let it get to me though, as it's only day one of my hunt. Something will surely come up.

Needing some extra emotional support, I arrive early to the stable to ride Buttercup before my shift starts. One benefit to working where you board your horse is you get to spend more time together. I try to ride him whenever I can. Someday, I hope to own a big piece of property where I can raise horses and let them run the pastures, but for right now, that's not possible. This is my best-case scenario.

Another good thing about working at the stable is Buttercup's boarding is free. It's a massive benefit, which I never take for grant-ed. I have wanted a horse my entire life and couldn't afford to board one. While all my friends saved for fancy cars or college, I worked all through high school, stashing every penny to be able to afford him. I was calculated when I applied for this job and expertly negotiated free boarding into my position. It was the win of a lifetime, and it allowed me to finally make my dream of getting a horse come true.

I jingle my massive set of work keys as I stride to the front gate and unlock the padlock, opening it just wide enough for me to slip through. I quickly shut it behind me. My riding boots kick up faint dust as the ground is so dry; it's like desert powder. It's wildly unnatural for Mapleton to not have snow this time of year, but this whole year's been dry. It definitely doesn't feel like Christmas is in less than two weeks.

I round the corner of the big center barn, spotting Buttercup in his outside pen with his giant amber head hanging over the wood fence, his wispy tail flicking to the side when our eyes lock.

That never gets old.

"Hey, buddy." I pick up my pace, right as a shadow appears in my peripheral vision. It's Don, my boss, and the owner of this place. He's not a regular business owner who hires people to do all the work. He's usually about somewhere pitching in and keeps busy maintaining a fence or forever cleaning pens. He's the hardest working boss I've ever had, which makes me want to work hard for him in return. "Morning!" I call over to him, slowing my steps as it appears he's coming toward me.

"Morning, Noelle." He lifts his index finger to the brim of his cowboy hat, flicking it just enough to tip it toward me. "Say, we need to talk before you take Buttercup out."

Halting my steps, I pause as my defensiveness kicks into over-drive. "If this is about Buttercup's ringworm, I already got medi-cine from the vet. He started it yesterday, and he should be getting better." Cringing, I still hear the angry clients calling me to complain about the massive outbreak, all thanks to him.

I just need a break. I pinch my lips together, waiting for the lecture.

"Oh, no." His gaze slides to my sweet Buttercup, who flicks his tail in anticipation of seeing me. "I knew you had that under control." His eyes shift to the ground, and then back to me. "I have some bad news. The landowner raised my rent quite a bit, and with the increased feed prices, I have no choice but to raise all the boarding fees. I'm sending notices out to all the clients this week."

"Okay." I nod as that seems logical. "I agree that's the best thing to do."

He shifts his weight from foot to foot in an uncharacteristic way. "Well, I hate to do this, but to minimize the rate increase to everyone, I need to tack on a small boarding fee for Buttercup. I'll give you a fifty percent discount, which I think we both can agree is generous, but he eats too. It's only fair."

"Fifty percent," I echo, doing the math quickly in my head. "That's four hundred dollars a month." My jaw drops as I automatically add in the extra grand I need to produce for Nate's rent, and at least another hundred for Nate's part of the utilities. That old farmhouse leaks like a sieve. My breathing ticks up, heaving out heavily as all the math problems I'm doing in my head circle around me.

It doesn't add up.

I make a measly thirty grand a year. I can't pay two thousand dollars a month rent and pay to board a horse on top of it. "Is there any way we can delay the fee until after the new year?" My voice is unusually high-pitched, but I'm hopeful—okay, at this point it might be a delusion—that I can find a side hustle so quickly.

"Well." He leans his head to the side, mulling the offer. "Tell you what. I can set it up to come out of your paycheck, pretax. It'll save you a few bucks, bringing the total cost down even more."

A few bucks?

I snort, and my eyes skirt back to Buttercup, who loyally whisks his tail my way. My heart cracks like an eggshell. I can't afford a horse if I have to pay for the boarding. It was always a stretch, but working here made it possible. I can get a better paying job, but then my boarding fee will double if I quit, and I wouldn't be ahead.

My gaze bounces back to Don. This isn't his fault. I've seen the feed prices ticking up almost every week. He's an honest man, who still outworks all his employees, even though he's in his sixties. He's right. Fifty percent off boarding is still a great deal. *Even if I can't afford it.*

"Can I work double shifts?" I already know the answer, but panic is seeping into my chest.

He regretfully shakes his head as he seems to instinctively know to take a few steps back. "I wish I could because you know we could use the extra help, but the overtime would kill me."

Don fades into the background, giving me my space as I stare at Buttercup. My legs wilt into mush, and my knees wobble, the thought of having to give him up is more than my heart can ever take.

First my twin brother leaves me.

Now I'm faced with selling my dear horse!

I need a roommate, at least until my lease is up when I can move someplace cheaper. *I don't know anyone who can move in by next week.*

Luke's chapped lips and his braces dripping in drool dance around my head.

Yep, there's nobody I know. I shake my head violently, wishing so deeply that it is true.

Nobody. Nobody. Nobody.

I turn back to Buttercup, who so lovingly waits for me. He doesn't ask for much, staying locked in a pen much of the time. All he wants is his muzzle rubbed, a daily ride, and a bucket of oats.

Tears prick the backs of my eyes.

I can't believe this is happening.

Nobody I know can move in.

Nobody.

But, actually there is *somebody* . . .

A whimper falls from my lips as the tears finally fall.

The agony over losing my best human friend, and now the prospect of losing my other best friend sends me into the darkest depths of panic where I didn't think I would ever go—to consider letting Luke be my roommate.

For no other reason than to save my horse.

Because he's all I have left.

There's only one way to do this.

I have to do it.

If I have any inkling of a chance to keep Buttercup and not become homeless, I need rent money next week. I can't believe I'm doing this. I suck in a deep breath and pull out my phone. There's no way I'm calling him. He can forget that. Instead, I construct a text to send to Nate.

Me: Hey, tell Luke rent is a grand and due next week. He'll need another 100 for utilities in two weeks. He can move in as soon as I have the cash.

I press send and close my eyes. The house is big enough for both of us. He can take a room downstairs, and I'll stay upstairs. It's only until I finish the lease, and I only have a few months left. Lesson learned about only having my name on the lease. I should have never let Nate talk me into that.

I can move in a few months to someplace cheaper.

I can keep Buttercup.

I open my eyes, a smile of relief tugs on the corner of each of my lips as I lock eyes on my dear sweet friend. Keeping Buttercup is my only goal right now.

A text comes back.

Nate: Done. He said he'll see you Monday.

I swallow, as this is becoming all too real, too fast. Whatever, what's done is done, and I can't take it back.

How bad can living with Luke really be?

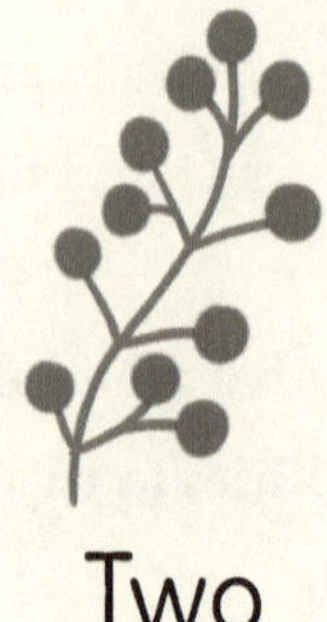

Two

Luke Halo

I stare at my phone, rereading Noelle's text Nate forwarded to me.

I've loved Noelle since I kissed her on a dare in junior high. I'd never kissed anyone before, and my nerves were twisting all my insides. Scared to death we'd lock braces; I definitely had more saliva than I needed when our lips touched. Something big happened. My heart got triple jujitsu flipped, and it has squeezed into a chokehold ever since.

Noelle is my Roman Empire.

The single person my mind wanders to whenever it's quiet.

But ever since that fateful kiss, she's acted very standoffish.

I get it.

It was cringe.

I certainly didn't sweep her off her feet the way I had hoped.

I can't believe Nate never suspected I loved his sister. Whenever he mentioned her name, I'd get all flustered. He must not suspect my feelings, or he wouldn't ask this favor. It's tempting. I don't mind living on campus, but helping Noelle out might give me the chance to redeem myself. I could spend real time with her and prove to her I'm not a metalhead with chapped lips anymore.

"Over here!" Mom interrupts my thoughts while waving me over to their traditional Sunday table at the Mapleton Country Club. It's the corner table, in front of a wall of windows, with views of the golf course and right below a picture of Arnold Palmer putting on the greens. When I was a kid, I used to beg to sit here, using it as an excuse to order the famous mocktail. I felt important getting that tall glass of lemonade and tea, the only time my parents allowed me to have caffeine. Now, this table is a twenty-year habit that never fell to the wayside.

"Mom." My lips pull into a teasing grin, and I set my phone on the table with Noelle's message still on my screen. "You don't need to direct me to the table anymore. I think I got it figured out by now." I pull out the tufted leather armchair and plop down, leaning back into the tension release that came with getting off my feet.

"I wasn't sure because they changed their tablecloths over to the red Christmas ones. I thought you might get mixed up."

"Well, considering they change to red tablecloths every year two weeks before Christmas, I think I wouldn't have panicked." I slide an hors d'oeuvre plate from the center of the table to rest in front of me and scoop myself a helping of the already served barbecue nachos.

Dad chimes in while lifting his water glass, "Did you get your civil law paper turned in?"

There it is, again.

I push my tongue to the roof of my mouth, digging for patience with my dad. He never takes even a moment to ask how I'm actually doing. Nope, he just wants to know about the stupid prelaw program—which I hate—so of course I'm not doing as well as he'd like. "I, ah, turned it in." My gaze is low on the nachos, and I'm pretending I need to remove all the pinto beans from my chip. I scrape them away one by one, doing whatever I can to deny eye contact.

"Well." Dad lifted a nachodelicious chip into his mouth, pausing to crunch down the size before swallowing part of it, finally completing his thought through a mouthful of food. "I talked to Dean Thornbrook about your C on the midterm. I told him you had gotten over strep throat and missed a couple of doses of your antibiotic. I offered to get a doctor's note for a retake. He assured me he'd talk to Professor Burns, as Burns clearly has it out for you." Dad shakes his head while tacking on, "This whole semester he hasn't given you anything higher than a B, and that's not going to work to get into Harvard Law School."

"Right." Since I've already pooled all the beans on a pile, and I still want to avoid eye contact, I move on to picking out the diced tomatoes, scooting them off the nacho mound with the prong of my fork. Dad always had an inflated sense of ego, unaware it might be my fault for not getting a grade higher than a B.

Because it is my fault.

Because I don't care about law.

I'd rather pursue carpentry, because I love working with my hands, but it's a little too humble of a career for my parents to accept. I could never admit that to him or it would kill him. His entire life's purpose since I was born has been to train me in all the ways to take over his law firm.

I intend to.

Law is a solid career path with a steady income. I can always build things as a hobby. I sigh, as it's unimportant today. "Hey, I think I know why I didn't get all A's this semester."

"Really?" My mom's Botoxed brows do that thing they do when they should rise. *Nothing.* "You have a reason?"

"Yeah, I think living on-campus is a distraction. My roommate is always noisy. I'd like to try off-campus living, and my friend Nate has a room opening. He said I could rent it—"

"I don't think that's a great idea," Dad interrupts. "Remember when you lived in that fraternity house for six weeks? It took me a month to convince Professor Brooks to let you retake your stats midterm." My dad clears his throat, and leans forward., "Say, speaking of off-campus housing, did you hear your cousin Rob got engaged?"

"Ah, that's nice." Like I care about his news. Our dads are brothers, and he's not likable. I don't keep tabs on his life, nor do I see how this affects my housing situation.

"Yes, and I'm not sure I ever explained to you the covenant that is attached to your grandmother Lily's chateau. I was waiting for you to get into your inheritance law class, because it's an excellent case study for that. It's always been a tradition on her side of the family that the estate goes to the first grandson to get married. I never wanted to encourage you to think about marriage before you were ready—especially since you aren't done with law school—but just so you know, when he gets the house, that's why. It's not because she loved you any less."

An alarm blares in my brain, sending adrenaline to speed through my body.

Rob is getting my grandma's chateau!

That house is so much more than a house. It's all my Christmases as a child. It's memories of sledding down the hills. It's toasty hot chocolate and even warmer conversations in the old kitchen. It's simple, handmade gifts lovingly set out by the fireplace on Christmas morning, and the kind and most loving smiles of my grandparents, while they were both alive.

My heart constricts into a hard knot in my chest, and I feel like I'm dying. Rob can't have my memories! I didn't care a lick about where I lived or Rob, but my grandma's chateau does not belong in Rob's greedy hands.

Not to mention, it sits perfectly in the middle of a hundred-acre forest, filled with mature maple trees, and healthy oaks. Grandfather had lovingly mentored me in how to care for the trees, as well as how to woodcut and build beautiful pieces of wood furniture. I have so many memories of being in those woods with him.

I started young, and I always knew that was my art—and my gift.

Wood being my art, and the time with my grandfather the gift. Now, it's the single place I use to supply my wood carving. I can obviously get wood from anywhere, but it just wouldn't be the same.

The thought of that house going to Rob makes my insides spiral into never-ending knots. My stomach hurts so intensely, it takes all my strength not to curl over. Rob is not the nicest person, and more than likely he won't keep the house in the family. He doesn't live in Mapleton and doesn't understand the importance, as he never spent any of his Christmases there.

There's no way I can let Rob have that house!

"Ah, that's interesting." My heart is thumping at the most random pattern. I'm clearly having a panic attack. My fork stops mid tomato slide, and my mind replays Dad's words. He might not think I'm as good of a lawyer as he is, but I'm awfully good at hearing what people *don't* say. I'm pretty sure he just told me *to get married first*, and I'll keep that house out of Rob's greedy hands. "I was going to tell you that I, ah, was thinking of getting engaged."

"Oh?" Mom sucks back a loud breath through pinched lips as she locks eyes with Dad. "That's quite interesting news."

Dad's lips bend into a hard wince. "We never heard about you even *dating* anyone."

"Yeah, it's a whirlwind thing, and like *so new*." I shift my gaze to a random crumb on the tablecloth and jiggle my leg under the table. I hate lying, but my panic pushes me to go on. "But it's interesting about the house. I wonder when Rob's wedding is." I thoughtfully tap my chin, pretending to not be making this up. "*Maybe...*I'll actually be married first?"

Dad's back noticeably stiffens as he sits even taller and clears his throat before saying, "I'm not sure what to think about this." His words come out with a heavy breath. "It seems awfully rushed, and we'd like to meet this lady. It's a big step."

"Right, such a big step," I echo. "But, if we get married first, would we get the house?" I toss up my shoulders, pretending to downplay my anxiety. "Not that it *matters.* Just asking."

Dad shifts in his seat and peers at me. "Yes, if you get married first, the estate will automatically be willed to you." He cocks his head. "What did you say her name is?"

"I didn't say what her name is." I tap my fingers on the table, and my gaze falls to my phone with Noelle's text face up.

It's the sign I need.

As soon as the lie had slipped from my lips, I knew who I would name. The only girl who owns my heart. Even if she doesn't know it yet.

"Ah, *Noelle.*" My heart skips a beat from speaking her name. "I've known her for years. So, it's not as fast as it sounds, and she's looking forward to meeting you both. Again. You know her from before."

"Noelle? Nate's sister?" My mom's neutral expression stays pinned on me, and all of a sudden I'm sweating like I'm being boiled alive. "I've always thought she had a pretty name."

I stare off into space, Noelle's face glowing in my memory. "Yeah, that's one of the many things I love about her." That's not a lie, as I love her name, and this is the first time I've expressed out loud any of my feelings about her. The verbal expression slaps the sweat on my low back, but unfortunately the hardest part of this conversation is still coming. I can't quit now. My gaze drops to my plate of nachos again. With all the tomatoes on a neat pile next to the beans, I have no choice but to start on the green peppers, sliding them over into a neat pile of their own. "So, that's great news about the house. Maybe I can talk her into moving the wedding up. You never know, we might be chateau owners soon enough."

Mom's eyes stay fixed on me, not unkindly. "That would be good, but first we need to meet her. *Again.*"

"Yeah, for sure. We need to set that up." My jittering leg is now pumping at full speed under the table, my calf muscle flexing and about to spasm. Above the table, I force a smooth motion to pick up my chip, devoid of all the veggies now, and drop it in my mouth with the mindfulness my mother insists on. It does nothing to calm my stomach. If anything, I've lost my appetite as my lie doesn't mix well with barbecue.

How do I break it to Noelle I can't move in with her?

Or how do I tell her the even better news?

We're getting married!

I'm not the smartest guy, but I understand the order of operations. No, not the scientific thing. This is the order of operations to deal with people. Before I say anything to Noelle, I need to take care of the bad news first, and I have a plan.

Whistling a tad, I stroll to the lobby and drop both of my palms to rest on the front desk as I direct my gaze to the residential assistant. "I need to fill out the form to have a guest."

The resident assistant is chewing on the end of a plastic drink straw and doesn't look up from his phone, as he grabs a single form out of the desk cubby and slides it to me. The form is stupid in my opinion. If we have guests for the day, they come and go, but anytime we want someone to stay for an extended period, we're required to fill out this form, which requests their basic information like name and car license plates. It's for security reasons or whatever, but I doubt anybody even reads them. I don't know Noelle's license plate, but the rest I'm able to fill out. I push the form back, and he receives it in silence, not even confirming the form is completely filled out.

Shrugging, as it's not my fault he didn't notice I left a space blank, I take this as a sign the roommate situation is supposed to happen.

It's time.

I'm finally going to be *seen* by Noelle.

This is the chance of a lifetime.

I'm not going to waste it. Once she's finally able to see me for who I really am, I don't have a doubt in the world she'll feel the same pull I do.

She might already feel it.

Who knows?

Maybe that's the real reason she's so standoffish around me.

I stuff my hands in my jacket pockets and whistle as I stroll out the door.

Destination: Noelle's.

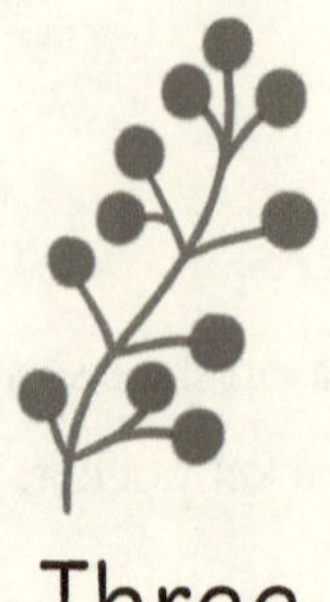

Three

Noelle

Waking up late, I roll out of bed at my usual Monday-morning-sloth speed. It's a workday for me, but Don knows I'm not a Monday person. We have an unspoken agreement that we don't talk about my Monday personality. If I make it to work by noon, he's good. I always work late to make up my time, often donating extra time after my shift.

I scratch my head, feeling the girth of my hairdo expanding around it like a clown wig. Even my hair knows it's Monday. I said goodbye to Nate yesterday, and it was amicable. I'm happy for him. It's been a while since he's had a girlfriend, and I want him to have a special companion, even if he left me in a terrible position. I pretended I'm fine with it all, even though it feels like a betrayal.

It is what it is.

After he left, I spent most of the day scrubbing his bathroom—blah—and bedroom. I cleaned out his snack shelf, making ample room for Luke, since I don't want him to encroach on my space. The only way I'll survive this situation is if Luke and I never have to cross paths. With last weekend being the downiest downer, it's still bleeding over into my Monday morning blues. I can't get out of this funk, but I force a deep breath.

On top of all this Mondayness, rent is due today.

I haven't heard a whisper from Luke since he said he'd be here today. Nate assured me Luke wouldn't fall back on his word. If I don't have a check in the rent box by five, I'm subject to a late fee. I've never been late for rent. I'm assuming my landlord will forgive one offense, but it's not a habit I personally want to test.

I slip my feet into my open-toed slippers and wiggle my toes until the bright pink toenail polish peeps out. The smallest things make me smile. As I stand, I find myself lifting the corner of my nightshirt to scratch my stomach. My stress has caused my skin to break out into itchy splotches. It's not a full-blown rash or anything hospital-worthy, but it helps add to my unsettled feeling this morning.

I lazily kick my gym shoes out of the way as I shuffle my feet toward the bathroom. I am about to reach for my phone—that's sitting on dresser because I couldn't find my charger to plug it in last night—when the front door buzzer goes off.

My stomach drops so fast, I practically hear a whistling noise like a bomb is dropping.

My gaze cuts to my alarm clock.

Who stops over at seven fourteen in the morning?

It's Luke or the landlord.

I can't believe I find myself actually praying it's Luke, because I don't have the money for my landlord.

"Coming!" I shuffle my slippers forward, hastily heading down the groaning wood stairs, making sure to skip the second to the last step. *That's the step that can't be trusted.* I meet the front door, placing one hand on the doorknob, and whip it open.

Just as I thought.

Slobberlips.

My shoulders dip, and my chin juts out in reflex, and I pause while I dry heave.

Even after all these years, I still feel the slobber leaking off my bottom lip.

It takes every ounce of my strength not to vomit. Unable to look at his face, my eyes hug the floor, where I see *no* luggage or boxes. My gaze bounces to the driveway, where his spoiled-little-rich-boy's Corvette is parked.

No trailer or truck.

Not even a trash bag of rumpled clothes.

"Where's all your stuff?" I mumble, my stomach twisting in alarm.

"About that." He scratches a spot on his cheek that's too dangerously close to his lips. Again, my shoulders tense, and I gurgle, fighting the ultimate cough. "So, my dad said I can't move in. I mean, I could . . . but he's not going to pay for it. Which also means he won't pay for my car, my credit card, school, or anything."

"What?" My jaw drops to the floor. "Why would you wait to tell me this until now!" I blurt out, heat flaming my face. "Rent is due today."

"Right." He wags his index finger at me, as if he's trying to interject into my coming rage. "I found another place where you can live rent free."

"You did?" My eyes shift from side to side, before I risk looking directly at him. I have to see if he's lying. I can almost safely plant my gaze on him. As long as I stay locked on everything north of his nose, I'm good. Hmm. That's interesting. He's got deep blue-green eyes that change hues right in front of my face. I'd never been able to make it past his lips before. Still, I hold my breath just in case. "Free is definitely in my price range," I ramble out, and Buttercup's sweet muzzle flashes through my mind.

I can handle free.

Free means I keep Buttercup.

This sounds too good to be true.

Nothing is ever *truly* free. "What kind of place is free? I'm not living in any place haunted or moldy. I don't do frat houses or live-in nanny situations either." My breath rushes in, but it's not bringing me any relief. I'm panicking. "You'd better not be joking, because my rent is due today—"

"Not joking at all." He flashes his palm to stop my near hyper-ventilation. "Look, I tried to get my parents to let me move in, but I lived off-campus my sophomore year. My grades dropped way down, and I got in trouble for partying. They still haven't forgotten about it. However, you're welcome to crash at my dorm until you find another place. And since they already pay for it, you shouldn't need to pay extra."

I blink.

"Whhaaaat." I stretch it out to be the longest one syllable word to ever grace the English language. "I can't live on campus. I'm not a student."

"It's not a problem." He offers an anticlimactic shrug. "I filled out a guest form. I think as long as we don't throw a loud party or anything, they will basically look the other way. My dad has most of the deans in his back pocket anyway."

"Wait a second." Ice frosts my intestines. "If I'm moving in with you, and my rent is due today, that means . . . I'm moving in with you *today*?" My gaze drifts back inside the house. It's mostly picked up from my massive cleaning yesterday, but nothing is packed. "I can't move today. I haven't talked to the landlord, and I need to get to work. I don't have time to pack."

"Relax." He lifts a reassuring hand, placing it on my forearm, and I hiccup cough this time. This cough is backed with stomach acid right on the base of my throat. I shiver as I hold in all the phlegm that wants to hurl out.

"If you can message your landlord," he thinks aloud, "I can take care of your stuff this morning."

My gaze wafts past him, back to his Corvette. It's black and silver, with fancy black rims, not so much of a speck of dirt on that thing. "Where are you going to load everything?"

"Um." He follows my gaze out to the driveway where it skips his car and lands on my truck. "Why don't we swap vehicles for the day?"

"You want me to drive your Corvette?" I blurt out, but a louder thought busts over the top of that one, a super-speedy thought I didn't even have time to think yet. "Why are you being so nice to me?"

His gaze swipes back over the yard, slowly drawing to mine. When our eyes lock, my swallowing reflex is immediately triggered. I grapple for the doorframe and hold on for dear life. There's a giant cough swirling in my stomach. It's slow, calculated, and crawls up my throat at the slimiest pace.

"Ah, Nate's always been a good friend to me." He drops his gaze to the ground, but carries on, unaware that something horrible is brewing in my belly., "And I feel like by helping you I'm doing him a favor." He tosses up a shoulder. "I'm sure it won't be for long, and you can find another place that is affordable—a few weeks, tops. By then, we'll be the best of friends."

My neck jolts, stretching out long like a crane, and a noise I've only ever heard in horror movies bleeps out of my throat. Not even sure what noise this is, but it starts from the depths of my soul. I'll call it a cackle*ish*-dying noise, mixed with a healthy dose of my-worst-nightmare-coming-true scream. "I'm not sure about that." I shudder at the mere thought of being anything more than passing roommates.

We definitely will not be friends.

I grab my throat, as it burns so deeply. I need to end this conversation before it turns lethal. Plus, the clock is ticking. Not only do I have to get to work, but I also need to call my landlord. I don't have time to come up with a backup plan. Against my better judgment, I swallow and drop my gaze to Luke's feet, because I can't risk looking at his face, and say, "Deal."

You better believe I'm spending all my free time scouring the classifieds for another living situation. A day or two—tops, and this nightmare will be behind us both.

Four

Luke

Noelle left for work, leaving me standing in her grandma-decor living room. It's not cluttered or anything gross, but I don't know how I'm going to pack up everything and still make it to my class by eleven.

Sometimes I need to not open my big mouth.

What was I thinking when I offered to single-handedly move her into my dorm? Where will I even put all this stuff? I'll need a storage unit at the very least. I survey the living room, furnished with a couch and loveseat, and a sprinkling of pink throw pillows. A large bookshelf lines the back wall, all stacked with color-coordinated books. Past the couch is the kitchen, and I didn't need to look inside the cupboards to know those are more than likely neatly filled too.

It's too much for me to move in one morning.

Can things ever go my way? I'm trying to impress the love of my life here.

Shaking my head, I roll up my sleeves and do what any red-blooded American man would do and pull out my phone.

There's no way I can move this furniture alone, but my room-mate, Boston, can come. He never goes to class. I take another deep breath, racking my brain for what I can bribe him with. Gritting my teeth, I press call on his name.

"Bruh," he answers on the first ring.

"'Sup?" I pace across the living room, forcing my tone to sound relaxed.

"Imma fixing to roll over and go back to sleep."

"Um, why don't you stop being lazy and get up? I need some help to move a friend in—"

"Nope."

"You didn't even let me finish."

"I don't need to hear the end of a sentence that starts like that. The answer to physical labor is always no."

"See, that's why you're so tired all the time. Why don't you get up and help me—"

"Nope."

"You can drive my Corvette for a week," I rush out.

"Nope."

"And I'll pay for all the gas." I throw that tidbit in because Boston's parents aren't rich like mine. He's a scholarship kid, and anything to smooth over his financial situation is sure to make this offer look better.

"Nope."

"You can drive it until the end of the semester."

Silence. Not just any silence. A hard silence, which says I'm getting closer. "You can drive it until the end of the semester. I pay for all the gas, and I'll treat Taco Tuesday every week from now until the end of the school year ."

"Aw." He sucks in a loud breath. I can feel it in my bones he's so close. Something is holding him back, and it's clearly not the car or he would have said yes already.

"Just tell me what your price is and get your butt down here." My fingers clench my phone tighter. He's too good of a friend to not help.

"Everything you said, but extend it until the end of the school year, and you got a deal."

"The end of the year?" My volume slides up. "Do you know what it costs to rent a Corvette for six months? And what am I supposed to drive?"

"It's cool. We can skip it."

"No, no, I don't want to skip it. If that's really your final offer, I'll take it." I bite my lip hard. This is a high price to pay for Noelle's love, but it's going to be worth it. Not to mention, Boston hasn't heard the other part. The part that explains *where* we are moving

Noelle to. As long as I get her stuff loaded and out the door today, the rest is mere logistical stuff. "I'll text you an address."

I hang up the phone and scan the room again, visually measuring the size of her furniture. There's no way we can fit this stuff in my small dorm room, but I can get a storage unit. I quickly scroll my phone, looking for numbers to call.

This is an awful lot to go through for a house, but it's not just that. Somewhere over the last day, it's become my second mission to help Noelle out. It's clear Nate is the one who should be helping since he put her in this bind, and I hate he ditched her.

The thing is though . . .

Men are fools when they are in love.

Clearly, Nate is a fool to leave Noelle.

And me, I'm a fool in love too.

And I have been for a long, long time.

I'm finally getting a chance to prove to her I can be that guy.

And when I convince her to go along with that other *minor* detail about the whole marriage thing, I'll get to keep my grandma's house.

It's a win for us both.

Five

Noelle

It's after dark when I jerk Luke's speed trap to a stop in front of the Mapleton college co-ed dorm. Mapleton's private college is on the edge of our small town, on five hundred acres of some of the prettiest land, which includes its own lake and golf course. It doesn't surprise me *this* is the college Luke attends. Everything about him is so out of touch with regular people.

Leaning my heavy head all the way back against the softest leather headrest, I listen to my landlord's speech on speakerphone. "You're technically breaching your rental contract to move out, and you're still liable for the remainder of the rent, but I can understand your financial emergency. I could take you to court, but if you move out today, I won't pursue anything legally. I'll keep your security deposit and, of course, the last month's rent you paid up front since I can't find renters this fast, and you're leaving me in a bind."

I zone out from his droning on.

If he's not going to take me to court, why bring it up? He just wants me to feel even worse. Wow, what a super nice guy.

I mean, I get that I signed a contract, but if I can't pay, I can't pay.

I'm desperate.

Evident by the fact I'm moving in with Luke Slobberlips.

"Ah, I appreciate your understanding," I cut in, defensiveness budding in my chest. "I'm sorry I couldn't do better."

"Might I suggest something?" His condescending tone makes my ears itch. "Most landlords aren't this nice, and behavior like this will get your credit history scarred fast. If I were you, I'd rework your spending. Try to make some more money and spend less. This type of reckless behavior will catch up to you later."

Reckless behavior?

My jaw quivers as I'm about to lose my mind. It was Nate's reckless behavior that got me into this mess. I bite my lip hard on that one. I guess it's my fault for not having Nate's name on the rental agreement. No point in arguing. He has no pebble-sized clue what I'm going through. I don't have rich parents like Luke does, who can just cut a check to finance their adult child's life.

My parents have struggled themselves, and the only thing they could offer is for me to move home. Moving back home would work, if I didn't have a horse to board two hours away. I can't afford to drive back and forth to work at the stable, which means I lose my discounted boarding when I switch jobs. I'll have to sell him unless I spend half my salary from a different job to pay for boarding, but I don't really get ahead that way. Plus, I'll be leaving him.

Leaving Buttercup will gut me.

What if he forgets about me?

Or worse, gets mad and resents me.

All my problems swirl around my head as I muster up a reply, "I'll, ah, put that on my vision board for next year." I'm only half-sarcastic.

"All right, Noelle, I think we're done with our conversation. You take care of yourself, and make sure to turn your key into the rent box, or you'll get another fee."

"Sure thing." I'm already searching for the end call button when I mutter, "Bye," and click. My eyelids crash down, and I tense until my whole body is so completely still I resemble a statue.

That was hard.

Inhaling, I slowly risk a deep breath, knowing only a minor fraction of my battle is over. That was the easiest part of my night. Next, I need to find housing I can afford, which more than likely isn't going to happen tonight. A more realistic option is to find another job and work myself to death to afford a shoebox apartment I can never be at, because I'm working all the time.

Such hopes and dreams I have.

I open my eyes, and nervously tap my thumb on the steering wheel.

What should I do next?

Don already said he can't give me more hours. Mapleton is a great little place to live. I love it immensely because it provides a nice rural place to have Buttercup, but it's not booming with employment opportunities. Most of the businesses here are family owned and only hire family members. I've asked around before, and nobody is hiring.

I could always come up with a business of my own, but what?

I don't have a degree or any actual real job skills. I only know horses, but it's not like people are lining up to ride those anymore. The industrial revolution pretty much destroyed that transportation model.

I slide my fingers to the door handle and crack it open, but my legs still don't move. I've hit rock bottom. I've been avoiding this moment all day, pushing the thought out of my mind. Now I'm here and must come to terms with the fact that I'm crashing with Luke.

Just for a night or two, fingers crossed.

A week tops.

It really can't be that bad.

My stomach sloshes around.

They aren't butterflies.

I'm not nervous one bit.

I'm afraid.

These are roaches with giant warning signs. I wish with every ounce of my soul I could heed those warning signs and squeal out of this parking lot, but at least for tonight, I need a place to sleep.

Pushing my elbow to pop the door wide open, my gaze falls woefully to the ground, and I trudge to Luke's dorm, vowing not to look south of his nose.

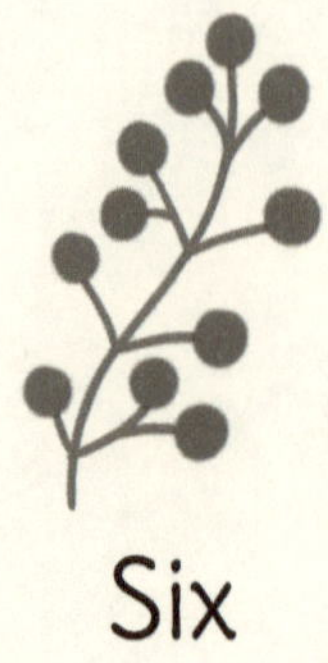

Six

Luke

"Boston," I pant out as I slide around the wood floor of our small one-room dorm on my stocking feet, gathering all the laundry. The place reeks like sweaty gym socks. I can't bring a girl back here. "You have to help me clean up. Noelle's going to be here any minute, and I still need to shower."

"Wasn't helping you move all day enough?" He's flat on his back on his twin bed, staring at his phone, moving as little as possible. He owns the left side of the room, and I own the right. We split everything right down the middle, including the window on the far wall. It's a micro-room, giving enough space for each of us to have a bed, dresser, and desk.

As far as accommodating Noelle, I've borrowed a guest cot. With only about a five-foot gap between our beds, I skillfully squeezed it in the middle. I stare at the humble cot, with the lumpy mattress. Even from a distance, I can tell it smells, and a single drop of sweat pulls at my temple. This is not the homecoming I would have loved to give Noelle.

She must know I'm trying!

"Get up and do something," I instruct. "This room needs to look like nobody lives here. I need this to look like *Disney on Ice* in ten minutes."

"Sorry to break it to you, but I'm fresh out of mouse ears." He shakes his head, letting his shaggy curls fall in front of his eyes. Boston has one of the alpaca hairdos that everyone but me has. I don't have it in me to carry on looking like a livestock animal. I've always strived to be clean-cut.

"It's just an expression." I don't add that's how my mom used to get me to clean my room when I was little, and I drop to my knees, pushing a Swiffer under my bed and mopping out four months of dust. I run the Swiffer under my desk and then jab the handle into Boston's side. "Take this and clean half of the room. I'm going to shower."

"You're going to need more than a shower to impress this girl." A snort bleeps out of his mouth. "When was the last time you even spoke to a girl?"

"Funny. I talk to my mom every day. Plus, I obviously spoke to Noelle today, or else how did I invite her over here? And who said

I'm trying to impress her? I've only been in love with her since middle school, but that's not that long."

Not sure why I rambled all that out.

That's interesting.

Like my words are stuck on auto-delivery.

That might be problematic. I swallow, open and close my mouth, and silently vow to do better.

"It's pathetic that you haven't made a move." Talk about not making a move, Boston continues to lie flat on his back, unhurried by my emergency. "Tell you what, you just open the door and surprise kiss her. Girls love that sort of thing."

"Uh." I wince hard, remembering the last time we kissed. It's not like I ever forgot it. "I kissed her once, but that's been sort of our issue. We can't get over it."

Boston cackles, drops his phone, and stares at me. "What the heck did you do?"

I strain my brows as far up to my hairline as they will go and swallow again. This oversharing must stop. "I don't want to talk about it," I grumble.

"If you implement my system, there's no way she can resist you." Boston shimmies his alpaca curls to one side of his head by giving his head a solid confidence toss.

"Your system?" I glare at him, as I don't have time to waste, and my heart is pounding out the seconds ticking on the clock. "What's that?"

"For starters, don't tell me you're planning on wearing another one of those V-neck polo shirts." The exasperation in his voice is growing, alerting me for the first time ever that someone might not love my fit.

I give him a stale expression. "What's wrong with my shirts?"

He jolts to a sitting up position. "Nothing's wrong for a health insurance salesman with a giant one-pack." He proceeds to stand and heads to our shared closet, whipping the bi-fold doors open. "The only women who will find this look desirable are the ones who are waiting for you to drop off a check from their dead husband's claim, and trust me"—he flips through my shirts, all neatly hung on hangers—"everything in this closet must go. You need a whole innovative approach." He slides his hand over to his side of the closet and grabs one of his vests and tosses it to me. "Trust me on this one."

"There's nothing wrong with my approach." I catch his vest as I slide in front of him, closing the closet door. "I can't change who I am."

"I'm going to help you out, but we need to work fast." He squares his gaze with mine. "First, how are you going to say hi when she gets here? And please don't do that prepubescent squeak."

I stuff my hands in my trousers, resisting his dumb question, but he glares at me until I eventually answer, "Ah, I'm going to say, Heeey, I'm so glad you made it here safely—"

"ERNT! Wrong answer." He waves his hand, as if he's clearing my words. "You need to be charming and self-assured, and not sound like you're a desperate little puppy dog waiting to be petted. Stand tall." He exaggerates his height and pulls his shoulders back.

"Smile, but use your eyes to say things your mouth isn't, and don't ever act like she's doing you a favor. Remember, you're the prize."

"That's sounds—"

Knock, knock.

That sounds like she's here!

My gaze slams on the door and I freeze.

"Don't panic." Boston sidesteps with swagger to the door, and whispers, "Be cool, because you *are cool*." He swings open the door, not even bothering to twist his lips into a small smile. "'Sup." He nods at her, barely making bored eye contact.

"Hi." She's wearing black cotton sweatpants and an oversized hoodie sweatshirt with her hair up in one of those messy buns that makes her hair appear curly. She always looks amazing, but something about her being in my dorm room makes my chest pinch tight. It could be her muted scent wafting through, bringing waves of something fresh and tropical, like I'm on an island. It's impossible to not inhale deeply when she's nearby. She flashes her palm in a wave while her other hand clenches around a small bag. "Sorry to impose. I promise I'll find something else as soon as possible."

"Not an imposition at all—" I lower my hand, ushering her forward, but Boston gives me a stony glare, and I cut myself off, and mutter, "It's cool."

Her eyes waft into the room, scanning the width in one small sweep. "This is . . . small."

"Standard, double dorm size." I take the three steps that are required to cross the room while gesturing to the cot. "Don't worry, I got everything you need for a cozy rest—"

Boston's glaring at me again, and I freeze. This is so much harder than I thought it would be. My palms pour out sweat, and my gaze bounces from Boston to Noelle. "Ah, that's my roommate, Boston."

"Nice to meet you, Boston." Noelle offers her hand, and Boston receives it.

"Same," he says in a gruff tone and drops her hand.

I hike a brow, wondering where his deep voice came from. I've never had a woman in our dorm before. It never dawned on me that Boston would act anyway but normal. My lips slug to the side, as this whole thing is cringe, but I focus on Noelle. "Um, I was about to take a shower. Ah, make yourself at home."

Her smile is sweet, but the dip in her head tells me more about what she's really feeling. My heart thrums so hard it reverberates in my throat.

I so badly want a do-over for us.

I'll do everything I can in these few days to help her see I'm not *as awkward* as I used to be. It's not even me.

This tension is more about her and what she does to me.

I know she wouldn't be here except she's out of options, and that must be hard for her. I definitely don't want to embarrass myself more, so I stay quiet, minding my own self while I slide along the wall toward the shared bathroom, already desperate for respite from her perfect scent. Her being here is going to be the biggest test I've ever had.

Upon returning from my shower, Boston's no longer in the room. He does that sometimes. More than likely he's on a late-night taco run. The dude has a serious addiction and depending on who he bumps into, he may, or may not, be back anytime soon.

I shuffle along my side of the room, sliding between the cot and my bed until I can plop down, phone in hand, ready to scroll. I'm giving Noelle space, not pushing her into conversation.

"Sorry again." Her enunciation is uncommonly slow, and when her gaze connects to mine, her eyes are glossy.

"N-No problem at all," I stammer back. I suppose this would be so much easier if I wasn't in love with her. My palms pour out sweat, as I ponder how to break the news of our upcoming nuptials.

I could just drop it.

She's been through enough.

Except, I haven't been able to get my grandma's chateau out of my head. I know with every fiber of my being that Rob will never care for it. He'll level it and sell it to some developer.

Well, that's not the whole truth. I have stopped thinking about the house, but only to think about Noelle before my mind slams back to the house and rebounds back again. It's enough to make me dizzy. "How was work?"

"Good." One corner of her mouth tugs into a sluggish, lop-sided smile. "It's always good because I get to spend time with my horse."

"You like horses?" It's a *dumb* question. She works in a stable. How much stupider of a question can I find?

"It's actually all I know and, frankly, is why my current situation stinks. Most people would say, just go to college, and get a degree, so you can have a stable career—"

"But you have a *stable* career." Apparently, I've moved on to dumb jokes. Now I'm left sitting in the vibrations of my words. "Sorry, didn't mean to cut you off. I couldn't help myself."

Our gazes crash, and she lingers on me for longer than I've ever seen her allow herself to look. Her blue eyes lighten before she lowers her lashes, beautifully hooding her eyes. "It's fine. I'm whining anyway."

"No, you aren't whining. It's great to hear about your life. Tell me about your horse." I set my phone down and turn, giving her my full attention. Boston's floating head appears in my mind, warning me to play it cool and not act this eagerly, but I right hook his head out of my memory.

Which is so satisfying, by the way.

"Buttercup?" Her gaze hangs on me overly scrupulously before I coax her again.

"Yeah, what's he like? Is he one of those easy keepers, or does he only like you?"

"You know about horses?"

"A little." I nod, adding thoughtful inflections to my tone. "My grandmother has an estate, just out of Mapleton city limits."

I don't tell her that someday soon, it'll be *our estate,* because I don't want to come off as a psycho.

But by withholding that tidbit, sweat beads on my brow. "It's set up for horses. Although my grandfather thought they were more work than anything. From time to time, they took some in, usually more as a rescue thing. I learned to ride a little. Course..." I tilt my head, cautiously slowing my words as I'm talking way too much about me, so I switch everything back to her, "That was a long time ago. You more than likely could teach me a lot."

That wasn't what I would have chosen to say had I not been so nervous.

Our gazes realign, my cheeks heat, but her gaze appears to soften. "There really isn't much to know. I think the main thing is taking the time to get them to trust you."

"Right," I blubber back, "trust is everything."

Her eyes slowly dance over my face, unlike her usual sweeping gaze that pushes me away. This one seems to silently challenge me to reveal all my secrets. "I'm talking about horses," I reiterate. When she doesn't reply, I tack on, "What else would I be talking about?"

"Well, it works for people too." Her lips bend into a hint of a mischievous smile. That's the rare one I've only ever seen right before our lips locked. Why is she pulling her pre-kissing smile out now?

It's causing my chest to pry open, slowly creaking into the silence. All the words I had tucked so gently away float out. Slowly at first, and I expertly trap them behind my tense jaw, but they are rascally and gain speed, ramming up against my teeth until my mouth drops open and I blurt, "Speaking of my grandma's estate, I'm supposed to inherit it, and it's great for horses. All colors of horses, and even big and short ones. It would be a great home for Buttercup. But as for the inheritance thing..." I—the biggest geek on the planet—proceed to not shut up—no, that would be too pleasant. Instead, I inject a point-making finger and continue to blubber all that should never be spoken. "There's a catch. In order for me to inherit it, I must get married before my cousin, Rob, and he's getting married any day. I love that place too much. I hate my cousin more than I love that place. And well, I had your text on my phone." I pick up my phone and flash the screen at her, even though the text isn't there anymore.

What am I doing?

Stop talking.

I don't.

I go on, and it gets so much worse. "Your text was looking so neat and distracting me, and I told my parents *we...*" I pause to laugh sarcastically. "You and I are getting married. But—" I cut my whole rambling off, and suck in a deep breath and tack on the last part before I die from an anxiety attack. "The good thing is, once I get the house, you could live there too, and now there's room for Buttercup, and well, we don't actually have to *get married,* because that would *be weird.* We could just say we did. What do you say—"

My words finally meet my ears, and they sound so frantic and desperate. Oh, it's so much worse than I could have nightmared up.

But I'm not done.

Nope.

Why would I ever cut this embarrassment off now?

I add one final pathetic plea, "Can you tell my parents we got married?"

I want to facepalm my head into my hands so hard, but I'm frozen, beholden to her as I hang on to her every breath, waiting for a reply.

I duck my head, and pray, "Please don't scream at me."

Seven

Noelle

I gawk at Luke as words pour out of his mouth. He hasn't said this much in the last ten years.

Where's the bottom of his word box? I tune him out, at least as much as possible in such a small room, but certain words cut through. Grandma. Inheritance. House. Buttercup. Marriage.

Wait. One. Moment. Here.

This is interesting in a run-for-your-life sort of way.

Marriage.

Why would he be speaking about that? My attention slams back enough to catch his eyes bulging out of his sockets as the last string of his sentence rings out, echoing in the silence. "Can you tell my parents we got married?"

"What?" My head jerks back. I might be missing a memory or two, because I can't fathom in what universe this makes sense. Then the door flies open, and Boston returns, holding one giant sack with a Ted's Tacos logo. We all take turns staring at each other, like this is a real-life *Whodunit game.*

"What's going on?" Boston strolls into the room, while reaching into his sack to pull out a foil wrapped taco. He tosses it to Luke, who catches it overhand and drops it to his lap.

Though his action is smooth, his words are terse. "I just accidentally proposed to Noelle, and you walked in before she had a chance to answer me."

"Ha ha." Boston pretends to laugh as he slips his sneakers off next to his bed, and retrieves another taco out of the bag, holding it up to flash it at me. "Want one?"

I'm quite hungry. The day has been nonstop, and the smell of chili seasoning and garlic are off-gassing from the sack, making my saliva pool in the center of my mouth. "Sure, I'd love one." I hold my hand out, waiting for his underhand toss. I catch it against my shirt, securing it for a second before I say, "Thank you."

"You bet." Boston reaches in for a third taco, unwrapping that one for himself, and takes a moment to peel the foil, leaving on the bottom half to prevent a mess. His overgrown mop of dark hair shields his face as he lowers his chin to bite into the taco. As he's chewing his mouthful of food, he pokes the elephant in the room. "So, what again about proposing? I thought you were still stuck on first base. I have to say, it's about time. You've been in love with her for like twenty years."

"Ten years." Luke's barefaced comment cuts through the air, adding to the throbbing tension. Heat floods my cheeks as his words sink in. I knew this roommate situation was a terrible idea. If I had even a cardboard box to flee to, I didn't doubt for a second I'd fly out this door, but it's December. I can't sleep outside.

Why is this happening?

I drag my gaze slowly over to him, dreading what's coming next.

Luke doesn't wait for me to reply. Instead, he abruptly stands, muttering under his breath, "Forget it." He opens the door and slips through it before slamming it shut in one swift motion.

My stomach drops as my mind recoils back to Boston's joke.

Luke can take a joke.

I've seen him laugh about himself before. He wouldn't get that mad over a silly jab unless there is something to it.

Everything started off sort of silly but got serious so fast.

I stare at the back of the door, my heart puttering against my chest wall as a thin veil over my memories pulls back.

I'm left with Luke's pretty bold confession.

He's been in love with me for ten years.

From the look on his face, I would say Luke was being dead honest. I fight the urge to let my jaw hang low, as I seriously had no clue he felt this way. Maybe I'm naïve, but this totally explains why he went out of his way to help me.

"I call dibs on Luke's taco," Boston says through another mouthful of food.

"You can have mine." Having lost my appetite, I underhand toss it back to him and roll over on my side. In a way, I'm glad Luke left.

It's mad cringe because I have nothing but ick feelings when I'm around him.

I don't have the slightest clue what to say to him. *Marry him?* The guy has totally lost his mind. First Nate went crazy and now Luke. What is happening to these men? Plus, I hardly know Luke. And I don't want to know him. How could he be in love with me? I've done nothing but avoid him.

My gaze slams to the heavens, wishing this was easier, but it's becoming clearer by the second I need to find a different place to stay.

I love my brother dearly, but I can't help but hate the position he put me in. While he's off gallivanting on the beach, I'm nearly getting brain damage from how hard I've been racking my brain for solutions. Short of living out of my truck, nothing comes to mind. I glance around the room, the sound of Boston crunching on his taco is escalating to piercing decibels. I cover my ears and hold back the tears.

I can't afford to work anywhere but the stable if I want to keep Buttercup and that means I have to stay in Mapleton.

I'm stuck.

My eyes skirt to the side, desperate for my phone. I need to check the roommate ads again. Something has surely come up in the last hour. Something, anything is better than this!

Eight

Luke

It's after midnight before I attempt to return to my dorm. Hoping Noelle has long since passed out, I tiptoe and gently close the door behind me. My plan is to sleep a few hours before I sneak out in the morning. My heart is slamming against my chest wall, telling me to stay so I get the rare chance to see her first thing in the morning, but I'm just so embarrassed, and this is making me crazy.

I blame Boston and all his talk about how I'm not cool for making me this flustered. I've never blubbered nonsense like that before. Everything went south so fast. I'm still willing to help Noelle, if she still wants to stay. I definitely don't think the three of us living in my dorm room will work though.

It would be perfect if we could get my grandma's chateau now, because we'd have so much more room. I press my index finger to my temple, trying to dull the stabbing sensation that's been there all night. I need to find a way to convince Noelle it's what she wants too.

It's so delicate because as much as I want my grandmother's estate for all the right reasons, I can't lay it all out for Noelle, because the worst thing that could happen is she feels I'm trying to use her. The whole way she got sucked into this mess was an accident. Truthfully, as much as I want that estate, *I want Noelle more*.

I'd live the rest of my life in a one-room apartment if it meant I got to wake up every day with her. Warm goosebumps race up my arms at the mere thought of seeing her first thing in the morning.

I do my best to quietly slide between my sheets and soft comforter. I flip my pillow twice before I find a nice cool spot to relax on, but I don't relax. My face is literally three feet from Noelle's, and the close proximity makes my adrenaline pump. I run my hand across the soft, fleece comforter, wishing it was Noelle's hair. As crazy as that is, I don't care. She's so close to me, I can barely hold myself back.

Oh, and then there's Boston's snoring, quaking out of the depths of his throat. He snores like he's part tractor, and it gets worse when he eats garlic. No idea why. It must have a cleansing effect or something. I'm not a scientist by any means, but I've witnessed this phenomenon so many times. I've thought an awful lot about it during the nights he's kept me awake. I've come to the hypothesis that all his bad eating habits congeal into this gelatinous mass inside his gut—possibly in his lungs too. When the garlic goes in, it dissolves the goo, breaking it all up into a loud, crackling mucus.

"I was waiting for you to get back.," Noelle's sweet voice calls to me in the dark, and startles me so much, I jolt and sit upright.

"What's wrong?"

"Nothing's wrong."

I hate I can't see her face. Except for a little sliver of light coming from the bottom of the window, where the metal blinds don't reach, it's pretty much black inside the room.

"I, ah, I'm confused about what happened earlier."

Ice rockets through my veins, and I fight the urge to crawl under my blanket and never emerge. "Um, me too." My tone sounds more incredulous than agreeable. I really don't want to talk about what happened. Thus, I stayed out all night. "We don't have to talk about it."

"I was going to tell you I appreciate you helping me out, but I think it's best I find another place to stay—"

"You don't have to do that," I cut her off, knowing I've made her uncomfortable, which was the last thing I wanted to do.

"Please don't take this the wrong way, but when you offered to let me stay, I assumed I'd have at least a couch in a separate living room." Her mouth is only a mere two feet from my ear. I'm able to focus on only that, despite the thunderous snoring wafting from the opposite wall as she continues, "I know it sounds naïve, but I didn't realize dorms were set up like this. There's clearly no room.

It's not fair to Boston, and three people living like this for a while are bound to drive each other crazy."

Perfectly on cue, Boston lets out the snore to end all snores. It rattles the thin windowpane, and I don't doubt it summons the dead.

"Is this about Boston's snoring?" I rush to explain. "It's only this bad when he eats garlic. I can try to control his diet—"

"No, it's not that."

My eyes are adjusting more to the darkness, and I can tell her face is bent down.

"That's fine if that's what you want." My heart twists, as it knows all the truth as to how I messed this all up. All I wanted to do was help her, but it's clear my talk of marriage pushed her away and why wouldn't it? "If I ask you a question, will you promise to answer it honestly?"

"Depends."

"Do you *have* somewhere to go?"

Silence drags out for so many beats I can easily count all the way to ten and back down again. "Noelle," I press, "I know you wouldn't be here if you had options."

"I can move back to my parents' but that makes my commute to work nearly pointless. The gas bill alone would eat up my wages. It's hard for me to think clearly as I'm still so mad at Nate for abandoning me." She shuffles her pillow noisily, moving it up and then back before taking it completely out from under her head, forgoing it to lie on her arm.

"Sorry if the pillow sucks. It came with the cot."

"I didn't say that." Her words sound pinched, as if she's holding back a giggle. "I just enjoy sleeping on my arm."

"Now I know you're lying." I chuckle. "Everything about these dorms is ancient. It's like they try to make us uncomfortable, preparing us for the 'real world.' If I had more time, I would have gotten you a better one." I pull out my pillow and toss it to her. "Try this one. It's goose down."

"I'm not taking your pillow." She tosses it back at me. "I've already made myself such an imposition."

Still holding the pillow square in front of me—like the perfect Little League catcher I trained five years to be—I pause. I was ready to toss it back at her, and start some pillow fight, but her words had pitched higher than normal, warning me of her sadness. "You're not an imposition," I say quietly. Not because I'm afraid to wake Boston. If he can sleep through his own snoring, he can sleep through anything. I'm careful not to pry too much.

"I am." There's a soft hiccup at the end of her sentence that reveals her tears.

"Hey, don't cry." I want so badly to reach across the narrow aisle of space between us and pull her into a hug, but I fear I'll only make her more uncomfortable.

"I'm sorry to be such a downer." She sniffs. "It's been an emotional week, and I wish things had worked out better. I think things aren't getting fixed until I admit I failed at living on my own and move back to my parents' home, which means I sell Buttercup."

Sniff, sniff. Hiccup.

"If you want to move home, then do that, but it doesn't sound like it's what you want."

"It's really the only option I have. At least for short-term options, but once I sell Buttercup, he's gone…"

My heart inflates to the size of a boulder.

Superman transforming.

I have another option!

"I threw a lot of words at you earlier, but what *if*—let's just think about it as an *if* while we work through this—what *if* you got to move to my grandma's chateau and *bring* Buttercup. You don't have to pay for any of it. You could still work at the stable to save money while you look at a more permanent solution—either employment or housing."

"You're actually serious about this?" She shuffles under her blanket before pulling herself to a half-sitting position.

"I'm serious about helping you, and I'm serious that I don't want Rob to get that house. So, yeah." I blow out an uneven breath. "I know it doesn't make sense, but if it helps us both out, what harm can it do?"

"So, what's the deal with the house?" Her words are measured and thoughtful. "You didn't really explain it to me."

"No big deal." I pause, as the truth of what that house is to me feels so corny to say. Like how can I explain hot chocolate tastes better in that kitchen? That sounds dumb. "Ah, I don't want Rob to get it. Plus, it's huge with plenty of room for us to live in. You'd be doing me a favor, so I'm happy to let you live there rent free until you find a better place." I drop my chin to my chest, as I worry about how to explain the next part.

Since I've already blown all my rizz for this lifetime, I speak honestly., "If you're worried about feeling safe, or it being weird, I promise to keep my space—"

"No," she cuts me off, "I get it. The thing is . . ."

I wait, counting the seconds, and when she doesn't reply after exactly twenty-seven, I interject, "What's the thing?"

"It's just, ah." She struggles between letting out a noisy sigh and squeaking out more words. "I hate lying to people, and it feels wrong to use you like that."

Use me, please!

I blink, so glad I finally managed to keep something in my mouth. See, Boston doesn't know what he's talking about. I have rizz. It just takes a while to warm up. "Like I said before," I continue cautiously, "we both get something out of the deal."

"Can I sleep on it?" Her voice is quiet, wavering.

"Sure." I drop my voice to a mutter. "If you can actually sleep with Boston's snoring."

Soft giggles waft out from her cot, but she doesn't say anything else. After a long pause—three hundred and sixteen seconds to be exact—I risk reaching out to set my pillow next to her head. Then I roll over on my other side, facing the wall to give her privacy.

"You don't have to give me your pillow."

"I know."

"Well, at least take my lumpy one."

Chuckling, I pull my arm under my head. "No, thanks, I'd rather sleep on my arm."

Quiet for another twelve seconds.

"Luke?"

"Yes, Noelle." The formality of using our names makes my heart slam against my rib cage.

"Thank you."

I lick my bottom lip, fighting all the words I want to say. I want to say it's the greatest pleasure of my life to be able to help you. I want to say, there's nowhere else I'd rather be. I want to say I think about kissing you again and again, all day every day, but instead I say, "Things will get better. I promise."

"I hope so."

I don't think she falls asleep, but she doesn't say anything else after that. I lie on my side, also fully awake, thinking about the fact she is only an arm's-length away. Never in any of my dreams would I have ever believed this would happen, and yet, there's a greater possibility of things getting even crazier in the morning.

What if she really does agree to say we got married?

Nine

Noelle

My eyes pop open with a jolt and dart to Luke's bed.

It's empty.

The navy blanket is neatly pulled all the way to the top, and my lumpy pillow rests on it. I scan the room. The bathroom remains dark, and Luke is nowhere to be found. My heart deflates as it recognizes he already left for the day.

Not that I'm missing *him*.

Even though he was sweet last night, and even a little funny.

I thought about his offer most of the night, and the unfortunate deal is . . . it's regrettably the only thing that makes sense. I can't stay in his dorm. I mean, it works for a few days—a week or two tops—but I'm going to wear out my welcome in this tiny space.

Plus, I have nothing to offer him back. I hate the idea of using him for a place to crash, but I'm actually using him more now, because he's not gaining anything.

If I'm going to take from him, I need to be able to give, and I don't have money to offer.

In the oddest of ways, helping him to get his grandma's house makes sense.

Hating all my options and hating this life where I must choose from the lesser of all bad options, I set my mind on returning the favor. I grapple for my phone resting next to me in the little cot, and text:

I'm sorry to put you in this situation. You are being too kind to me, but if the offer still stands, and you think your parents will allow it, I'd love to move into your grandma's house.

I stare at my phone screen, waiting for a reply, but after a few minutes, I decide he's busy. Cautious to not wake Boston, I get up to tiptoe to the shared bathroom, ready to start my new life.

Okay, I might have whimpered a little.

When I arrive at work, Don's nowhere to be found. I take the opportunity to hang out with Buttercup, preparing him for his big move. "Okay, buddy. Here's the deal." I rub his ears the way he likes it, and his jaw opens in delight. "I know you like it here, but some things are happening which I can't control. I don't want to stress you out with the details, but it looks like we both need to move, but"— I rush to get the good part out— "we get to move *together*, which is amazing. We are going to live in the country, and you'll have a nice big field. I'll make sure to bring all the oats, and maybe we can even get you a new bridle. You know, one that fits better around your ears. I should have money for stuff like that if I'm not paying so much for rent. At least for a while until I find a new place."

Of course he doesn't utter a sound, but he flicks his tail and allows me to continue to rub his ears. That's a good sign. My phone vibrates in my pocket, and I pull it out with my free hand.

Luke: I'm figuring out a way to break this to my parents. I think the only way it will work is if they actually get a chance to talk to you, and the sooner this all happens the quicker we can move. Would tonight work for dinner at their house?

My breath grows shallow, and I stop mid-rub, needing to rest my hand on the fence for support. This is all happening so fast. I have to hang out with Luke, and now we're involving his family.

Is this really what I want to do?

Before I can answer myself, Buttercup pushes his muzzle on my hand, bumping it back up on his nose, hinting he wants me to rub him more. And that's the thing. The arrangement with Luke is the only way I can keep Buttercup, and I don't have the option to mull this over again. I quickly text back:

Me: Sure. Just tell me what I need to bring. I get off work at five. Any time after that works for me.

Luke: You don't need to bring anything. I'll talk to my mom about the time, but I'm sure we can head over as soon as you're free.

Me: Great.

Luke: Talk to you later.

Oh, the things I do for my horse. I sigh and wrap both arms around his neck, pressing my face into him, feeling the hug deep in my soul. He's the *only* thing that makes this insanity worth it.

I dart out of the dorm bathroom and scurry to my overnight bag to riffle for some makeup. Working at a stable makes me a minimalist when it comes to any makeup and my hair routine, but it's not lost on me how important it is for me to look like I care about meeting Luke's parents—again. I've met them in passing plenty.

This is different.

This is me playing the part of someone potentially coming into their family.

Warm goosebumps dot my arm as this whole scenario plays out in my head in the most absurd way. With more warning, I might have picked up a fresh lipstick or something festive, but all I find in my makeup bag is my plain beige eyeshadow and peach lip gloss. It's about as natural of a makeup look a girl can get, but it'll have to do. I pump the wand on my lip gloss several times, as it's almost down to the bottom, and begin to apply it to my bottom lip when the door opens.

Luke walks in wearing dark trousers and an insulated vest, like all the preppy boys wear on campus. His hair is smooth and brushed back above his ears. It's that old-money haircut you see in all the New England states. A perfect eighty-twenty part.

I pause mid gloss application.

My gaze hangs on his vest.

Usually when I've seen him, it's on the weekends when he hangs out with Nate, and they're doing dumb boy things like gaming. He's usually in a polo shirt. I've never seen him dressed like this before.

It's a very nice vest.

It gives his shoulders weight-lifting vibes.

"Hey." His lips bend slightly at the tips as he takes a step inside, keeping a hand on the door. "Are you ready to go, or do you need a few minutes?"

I stick my lip gloss wand back in the tube and close it tight before I stuff it in the zip pocket of my oversized wallet purse. "I, ah, should be good." I strap my purse on my shoulder but pause to check my jeans and sweater ensemble. "Unless you think I should change?"

Without missing a beat, he shakes his head. "You look great." Our eyes lock, and a wave of heat creeps over my cheeks before I turn my gaze toward the door while he tacks on, "You always do."

It's odd.

Luke's always been nice to me, but I guess I never allowed it to sink in because of how embarrassed I'd been.

Oh, wait a second!

That is weird.

My eyes flash side to side. My reactions around him have totally calmed, because I haven't had one cough since I got here.

I wonder what changed?

I've been trying to stop it for years!

Am I really healed?

Wow, things are getting weirder every day. A shiver runs up my spine, but I shake it off and step in line with him for the door. "We can go."

"I'm thinking about what we should say." He hangs back, holding the door open while I pass through it, and then pulls it closed behind him. We fall into an easy stride together as we pass through the long hall. "My parents are going to have questions."

"Right." I swallow, thinking about all the questions I still have, even though I'm part of this whole thing. "I think we can be honest that we've known each other for years, as that part makes sense. Don't you think?" I turn toward him, checking his facial expression. It's easy and neutral.

"Yeah, they understand the enormous amount of time I spent at your house, but they are going to want to know more of the timeline about how long we've been *together*, especially since we're supposedly talking about marriage already. I didn't give them any details yet, because I wasn't sure what you are comfortable with."

"Well." I purse my lips as we've made it to the exit, and he holds the door open while I go first. "Maybe we keep it ambiguous. Like it's been gradual, but we finally decided, since it's your last year of college, it makes sense to get engaged now so we can plan next year together."

"I guess that could work." He walks up to the driver's side of his car, while I round the corner and find the passenger door unlocked, and we both get in.

He cranks the engine but pauses to scratch an itch on the side of his face, and I marvel at how I can actually look at him without coughing.

It is a humongous relief.

I relax in my leather seat and listen to the music that plays softly out of the car speakers. He puts the car in reverse and looks over his shoulder, passing a smile at me before saying, "So, just so I know you understand the agreement, I have to actually *get married* to get the house. Yes, we aren't going to do it, but the sooner we *say* we got married, the sooner we both move."

"Right." I curtly nod. "I got it."

His Adam's apple slides up, before relaxing back down, and for the first time, I wonder if he's a little nervous about all of this.

I've always known he has one of those minds that's logical and thinks in a linear pattern, having a solution for everything. Even with Nate, Luke was the leader of the two, and there's something trustworthy about him.

Even before he put on the vest.

The vest just enhances it.

We drive the two hours to Richmond, where Luke's parents live and where I also grew up. As far as I know, Luke, Nate, and I were the only ones from our high school who moved to Mapleton, and I love it that way. I feel like I have gotten to reinvent myself. It's not like I didn't like who I was in Richmond, but growing up with a low income, I just felt there was a stigma that followed me when I was with my peers.

For this reason, I don't go back to Richmond very often.

I watch out the window as the weather has drastically shifted, bringing in low hanging gray clouds that mask the sun. Luke's parents live in a gated community, one where the longer you drive down the road, the road gets more winding, the bushes get taller, and the yards get longer. It's a lot different than how I grew up, lower-middle class. I always found it odd, even though Luke was the one with the giant pool in his backyard, Luke hung out at my house more than his own. He claimed his parents were strict.

I guess it made sense.

When he pulls into his long circular private drive, and parks in front of the door, I'm ready to stretch my legs. I quickly climb out of the low-riding vehicle and glance up at his parents' red brick home. It's a commanding house, with two huge white pillars framing the door in a perfect Colonial-era façade. I'd only ever been in the driveway, either dropping or picking up Nate, but I've been curious to see behind the walls most of my life.

"Are you ready?" I didn't hear Luke come up beside me, but he's standing close enough to me now that I can smell his aftershave, fresh and crisp with notes of iris and musk.

"I think so." We take the front steps together, and just before Luke reaches for the door, he grabs my hand, swiftly linking his fingers into mine.

He gives me a look of encouragement. "We're going to have to play the part."

"Right." I wiggle my fingers to rest comfortably around his, and suck in a lungful of air. It's really not a big deal. Just an hour or two, and I get to keep Buttercup.

I get to keep Buttercup.

Luke whips the front door open, and he waits for me to walk through it. With the large entry hall floors being marble and the cathedral ceiling stretching tall, the door shutting behind us echoes, which is immediately followed by what sounds like heels clicking from down the hall.

"Luke, honey, is that you?" Mrs. Halo's voice rings from the stillness down the corridor. I lean on one foot, trying to nonchalantly peek around the corner, the old house seems to come alive once past the entrance. Christmas lights and evergreen garland frame much of the grand staircase, and poinsettia plants dot each stair.

Luke silently nods me forward, and our footsteps join on the marble. We reach the end of the hallway before I see Mrs. Halo, my heart pounding in my chest. She's dressed in a fitted cream pantsuit with a blazer. Chunky gold chains wrap around her neck and wrists. With her honey-blond hair curled perfectly to flow down her back, she is truly a woman of elegance.

I immediately wish I'd opted for a dress, but it's too late now, as Luke ushers me forward. "Mom, you've met Noelle before."

"Yes." Mrs. Halo's brow is still but holds a supernatural power to pin my feet to the floor. "Welcome, Noelle."

"Thank you." My lips hardly slip over my teeth, so I part them to force an open-mouth smile. "How are you?"

"Very well." Her curt answer does nothing to calm the quibbles in my gut. "Please, come have a seat. Hors d'oeuvres are already served."

Luke drops my hand, immediately wrapping his arm around the small of my back, and pulls me to his side to whisper in my ear, " *Relax.*" Gesturing with his head across the hall, he guides me to the dining room, dimly lit with an overhead chandelier and four candlesticks on an elongated table. Fragrant cinnamon sticks and dried oranges fill a platter in the middle of the table, tying my attention to it.

"Everything looks and smells so lovely." I shuffle my feet forward as Luke guides me to the table and slides out a seat for me. I've never had anyone pull out a chair for me, and I'm stiff as I resist the urge to plop down, instead lowering myself neatly.

Luke sits next to me as Mr. Halo comes through the back entrance, wearing a crisp black collared shirt and dark slacks to match. He has the same blue-green eyes as Luke, and his smile is more generous than Luke's mom's when he greets me. "Nice to see you again, Noelle."

"You too." I trap my lower lip between my teeth, as I wasn't prepared for this formal dinner. At my parents' house, we eat at a round table, with mismatched plates, and all chatter and talk over each other. Here, I'm afraid I'll get a time out for speaking out of turn, and I hold my gaze on Luke, waiting for all the clues.

Mr. Halo pulls up his chair at the head of the table and reaches for a plate of crabcakes, serving them onto the small round plate in front of him, before passing it to Luke. "So, Luke," he starts as soon as Luke takes the plate, and he picks up his fork. "How did your paper on Juvenile Justice go? I trust you turned it in on time."

Luke plates a crabcake for himself and passes the tray to me. "Yes, sir. I turned it in but haven't heard what my grade is yet."

"Did you mention that I served on the panel for the Richmond Juvenile Justice Defense Committee?" Mr. Halos swipes at his patty with his fork.

"I couldn't find a way to work it in, as we were instructed to only use peer-reviewed journals and not interviews for this one." Luke grabs his stemmed water glass, taking several swallows. Their conversation feels more like a job interview than dinner chat, making my position as a bystander uncomfortable. "If it's okay, Noelle and I want to talk about something." Luke's gaze hovers over mine as he reaches over, resting a hand on my leg. My gaze drops to his hand on my knee, and I marvel again how he can touch me without it creating that dry heave thing I used to do. Something strange is happening . . . Luke's lips curl into a genuine smile as he goes on, "Noelle and I, we're—"

Knock, knock.

"Ready for the main course?" His mom jumps out of her chair and starts chattering over the top of Luke as she heads out the side door. "That's the caterers, and just wait until you see what I ordered. It's Mongolian. The veggies are to die for."

A look of disgust washes over Luke's face as his gaze turns back to me. Fire flames my cheeks. She had to know the announcement is coming. Luke told me he prepped them.

My gaze falls to the side, and it hits me like a bus without breaks. *She doesn't like me.*

But she doesn't even know me.

Therefore, she's judging and likely doesn't think I'm good enough for him. A fire ignites in my gut, fueling anger to bubble up.

I know I'm not the country club type, but I could be *good enough* for Luke if that's what he wants. My gaze bounces from the doorway, back to Luke, and his lips are parted, but he's looking down at his plate again.

He has to know what happened is because of me, and now I feel bad. Like he went through all of this trouble to help me, and he's going to take heat from his parents. What if his mom actually talks him out of it?

I could lose Buttercup.

The stakes just doubled, and I'm feeling the pressure to start the hard sell. I place my hand on top of Luke's and smile at him. Not a fake smile, but a we-*are-in-this-together* smile, and I vow through pinched lips to make this performance a huge success.

After the lightest dinner ever, as I'm not even close to being remotely full, Luke and I meander into the all-white living room for after-dinner conversation with his parents. Evidently his mom decorates the whole house with Christmas decor, and we pass another tree near the large stone-white fireplace on the way to take seats on the sofa in the center of the room. I sit in the middle, while he continues to the end, plopping down before eyeing me in the middle. In unison, we shimmy toward each other until the space between us narrows and now we are snuggled up next to each other, doing our best to look like a couple.

"What did you decide about your Ethics class?" Mr. Halo takes his seat on the white leather armchair closest to the fireplace. He methodically pulls out a stick of gum and tosses it into his mouth before tacking on, "Are you going to write your paper on capital punishment like I advised?"

"Dad." Luke rubs at the back of his head, squinting as if he has an annoying itch. I don't blame him. It's been nonstop drilling about his law classes since we got here. "I'm glad you are interested in my future, but there is more than just school. Noelle and I have something we want to talk—"

"Hot chocolate, everyone." Mrs. Halo appears in the doorway, carrying a tray of white mugs with steam piping out of the top. "It's made from imported Belgium hot chocolate bombs. They are the best I've had." She lowers the tray to the Art Deco coffee table and lifts two mugs off the tray, turning toward us. "Oh, did you notice you were under the mistletoe?"

"Mistletoe?" I giggle nervously, scanning the room as I don't notice anything.

"Yes, I wanted a little something festive. Looks like you two have to kiss." She motions to the vaulted ceiling, where a sprig of something green peeks out of the center. It looks so oddly out of place, and I squint as it comes into focus.

Yes, it is mistletoe.

Aren't those supposed to be in doorways and have huge warning signs?

My shoulders cinch together in a giant cringe. I understand I'm pretending to date Luke, but this is only our first time hanging out as a fake couple. I hadn't even thought for a moment we'd ever have to *kiss.*

I glare at the mistletoe as it seems to throb in warning. Heat flames on my cheeks, and I count the seconds, wondering how long I can stare at it without having to face Luke.

A good solid minute. I hope.

My stomach quakes. A flashback of middle school plays in my head, and I can't believe this is happening again.

And in front of people.

I could run.

Oop, there it is.

The return of my dry heave.

Nothing about this is going to be good.

"Mistletoe," I whisper, gasping for air as if I'm crawling out of a war trench. My gaze finally drops to Luke, and I pinch my lips together, preparing for the worst. Horror music plays in the background of my mind and every hair on my arms stands up straight.

"Actually, it's perfect." Luke stands up before I can do a lean-in, and I heave a giant sigh of relief.

But that's wrong!

I should not be relieved.

Something so much worse is happening!

"I've been waiting for the perfect moment, but we keep getting interrupted, and this has to be it." Luke slides in front of me and reaches his hand into one of the vest pockets, pulling out a velvet box right as he drops to one knee!

My chest cinches tight.

Then cinches again.

I could protest, but I'm so massively confused.

Mrs. Halo lets out a gasp, similar to the one that's clogging my throat with a death grip of terror, while Luke opens the box.

A ring.

Not just any ring, a rose gold band.

"What are you doing?" I whisper, a little harshly, the ring pulsating in my peripheral vision.

"We talked about this, remember?" His voice drops, rasping.

"We talked about *marriage*." I tilt my head to one side, as if I'm physically dividing this argument in half., "But not *this*, and not in front of *them*."

"You're being modest." He laughs, tossing a look back at his parents. "I thought it would be nice to share this moment with them."

"You did?" my voice squeaks, as I'm totally blindsided and wishing I had at least a heads- up. The arrangement had sounded so much more business casual than what's going on right now. A proposal on one knee is not business casual. This is my heart in my throat, and I'm about to throw up. "Where did you get a ring?" I hiss.

"I bought it today."

"Today?" I grapple for my throat, praying something gives before I pass out. Or worse, my coughs return with vengeance.

"Yeah, today when I was thinking about *you.* "

Doing a hard pause on the word, *you*, he's still holding the ring awkwardly in his hand. I frantically search his face for signs of a prank, but he doesn't have an ounce of humor curved into a smile.

He's one-hundred-percent serious.

Quakes rumble against my rib cage. This is an act. I'm clearly about to blow our cover as I'm acting so confused, but this whole thing is blowing my mind. "This is happening so fast."

"It's okay. Better than okay." He takes my hand in his, holding it in front of him. "Ten years ago, you kissed me on a dare. You didn't know it at the time, but I was already falling in love with you. You were my first kiss, but I knew in that moment, I wanted you to be my last."

I blink. Everything about his proposal sounds *genuine*.

My gaze floats to his mom; her hands clasp together in front of her, but her gaze is piercing in my direction. Luke's dad has a *that's-my-boy* grin laced on his lips.

And Luke!

Luke's winning an Oscar for his acting. His gaze dials right into mine, like it's boring a trail through my eyes right to my heart. I can't even tell it's a fake proposal, and I one-thousand- percent know it's fake.

It is fake . . . right?

This isn't what I had in mind when I considered this whole fake marriage thing, but I get it. He's trying to convince his parents, but I struggle to stop my tears from welling up as these emotions—*totally fake emotions*—clog my throat. "Luke," I whisper with a shaky breath. I need this scene to be done. Seeing him on one knee, holding my hand is burning a memory into my brain—*one I desperately don't need.*

"It's okay." His voice is a tad hoarse but steady. "I need you to know how I feel about you."

"I know," I whisper.

He tilts his head like he's about to add a rebuttal, but his lips pinch together, and after a moment, he lowers his gaze to the box. When he raises the ring in front of me, he tacks on, "I want to be the person you make all your best memories with." His eyes are potent, spiraling flecks of light back at me as his voice drops into a deep octave. "*Marry me, Noelle.*"

Hearing him say my name like that sends a beam right through me, and goosebumps run all up my spine. I'm not sure where the tears come from, but I can't blink them back. A single, warm droplet falls to my cheek, and I nod my yes as my words are broken.

Luke raises his brow, leaning in, waiting for words, and I try again to squeak something past my emotions and finally manage a breathless, "Yes."

A smile pours onto his lips as he slips the ring on my finger and springs to his feet, wrapping his arms around me. I jolt from a spark that zaps me into a stillness. I hug him back, stiffly at first, but he wraps his arms tighter around me. He's a head taller than I am, and he lowers his head to my neck, and I lean my head back right as he presses a kiss to my lips.

I wasn't prepared for that!

He's definitely not Slobberlips this time.

In fact, they are quite the opposite: warm and soft, like melting butter.

Silky Butterlips is more like it. Tingles erupt in my core, rippling out, and I feel the reverberations in my toes.

I get it.

We just got engaged.

Sort of.

Hypothetically.

He's playing the part.

A little too well.

I didn't think he'd sneak one in there though.

I'm frozen, basking in the tingles, when his mom rushes over to hug us both. I'm grateful she's one of those huggy people who has no personal space, because I need someone else in my personal space. Someone to take my mind off Luke and the tingling still vibrating from his nearness. Yeah, I fold my lips in, pinching them tight. I need to put an immediate stop to the tingles.

No good can come from that.

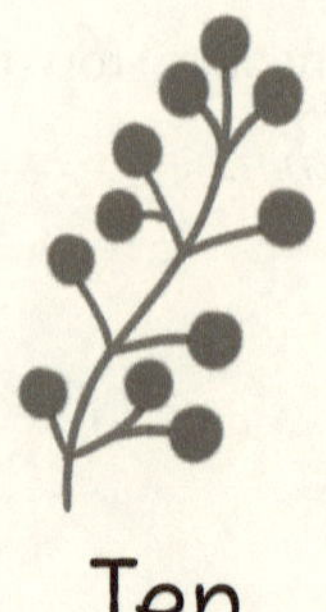

Ten

Luke

My flesh is boiling so much my palms pour out sweat as Noelle and I finally hug Mom and Dad goodbye. As soon as we tuck safely inside my car, with both doors closed, Noelle's gaze frantically hooks on mine, and she screeches out a horrid sound. "Have you lost your mind? You proposed!"

I can't tell her, not only have I lost my mind, but I lost my heart to her many years ago, and apparently, this whole charade is making me come undone. "Sorry." I start the car and pretend to be overly focused on steering the car out of the circular drive. "I knew they'd never buy the whole marriage thing without proof. When I went to get a ring, the idea just popped into my head. Since

Mom and Dad refused to let me talk to them about our marriage, I decided to do something drastic."

"Popping the question doesn't just *pop* in your head." She refuses to close her mouth, and I can see all her perfectly aligned molars. At least our kids won't need braces.

Ug! Stop it, heart! We aren't getting married for real. There will be no children.

"Sure it does. That's how they got the phrase 'pop the question,'" I tease. My brain knows it's fake, but my heart heard her say, "yes" to my proposal. I've been floating, apparently so high I'm bumping my head on the ceiling to the point of delusion. How will I ever recover from seeing the love of my life—yes, she's a secret love but a love nonetheless—say she'll marry me. It took every ounce of strength I had not to whisk her in my arms and kiss her until we were both breathless.

"I don't think I'll ever get over that," she pants out, holding her chest. "I have to be able to trust you. So, if you get any more ideas like that, you must let me know ahead of time."

I'll never get over that either.

I squeeze the steering wheel, avoiding looking at her and her perfect molars, because I'm already starting to name these imaginary kids who won't need braces. At least two. If we continue the N theme of her name, I like Nora or Nyla for our girl. A boy, definitely Nash because it's tough.

What am I doing?

I nearly slam my head on the steering wheel.

This is torture.

My heart seriously won't shut up.

It believes I'm marrying Noelle.

"Look." I pause, sneaking a look at her, and my heart putters so fast against my rib cage, I'm glad I'm sitting. "Since we aren't going to have a fake wedding that my parents can witness, they need something to believe this is real. It seems like a hassle, but trust me, in the long run, it will only help us get our house faster." I pause with an apology on my tongue, but it won't come out.

Did I take it too far?

Maybe.

Can I say I'm sorry?

I really can't.

Maybe I'll be sorry later when this whole charade is over, but seeing her agree to marry me was everything I'd ever wanted. If I can't have my dreams come true for real, it is worth it just for a night. "I'm *not* sorry," I affirm. "It's going to be great."

"So, now what is your great plan?" She flicks her palm out as if in question. "You need to tell me everything."

"Honestly"— I take a left turn, get into the fast lane, and adjust my speed before I continue my thought— "my dad's a lawyer. He's not easily fooled. We're going to need proof of a wedding."

"So, we need to fake some photos or something?" Her eyes narrow into concentration slits.

"No, my dad knows all the judges in the district. We'll never be able to say we got married. I think the best thing to do is go to Vegas for the weekend and save all our receipts, because Dad will audit my credit card. We come back 'married.'" I insert finger quotes around married to indicate it's all going to be a farce.

"I can't go to Vegas!" Her jaw dramatically flops down. "I can't even afford normal rent. Vacation is not an option."

"Right. That was before." I wag my finger to the left, foreshadowing a change of direction. "I'm your husband now, so I'll pay for that."

"And by that, you mean your parents will pay when they get your credit card bill?"

"It's all fine. My dad expects it, and trust me, he'll get more than what I owe him when I start working for him. It's his long-term investment strategy."

"I don't know." She sucks in a loud breath before letting it out slowly. "I think we might have gone too far with this. Maybe I need to look for a new place to live?"

"It's fine," I rush to calm her rebuttal, as now that my heart thinks we're engaged, I honestly can't entertain the thought of rethinking this. At least not tonight. "Tomorrow, we'll fly to Vegas, stay the night, and come back the next day. The official story is that we were so excited to be engaged, we couldn't wait. Since I have finals next week, we only took a day. We're planning a bigger wedding for this summer. Then we spend the semester together in the house, and we can talk about our *b-breakup* later." I stutter on the word breakup. It stings. I pray with every fiber of my being that Noelle will develop genuine affection toward me. I'm going to do everything I can to get her to see that not only have I loved her since we were kids, but I am worthy of her love too.

It's my one shot.

I've never wanted anything more in my life.

"If you think it will work." She nervously nibbles on the tip of her thumbnail, scrunching her nose the way she does when she's worried.

"I'm confident it will." I don't even hesitate before I tack on, "I mean, what could possibly go wrong?"

Her head jolts back and her eyes lock in a haunted stare. "Don't you know you should never ask that question?"

I swallow, a low chuckle brews in my throat as she has no idea of the plans I have for her. If I have my way, nothing will go *wrong.* Everything will be completely right, finally.

Eleven

Noelle

How long are lip tingles supposed to last before it's considered a dire medical condition?

I lie—fully awake—tucked between a scratchy sheet and a cardboard*esk* blanket, a mere foot from Luke—well, to be fair, I'm also two feet from Boston too, but my body doesn't share the same awareness to him—feeling these lip tingles.

Luke's deep measured breathing tells me he's sleeping well. After each inhale, he lets out an adorable little sigh of an exhale.

Did I just consider Luke adorable?

My throat cinches, but instead of it hurting, the sensation sends off another round of tingles.

This cannot be happening!

I wish I could sleep, but nope.

These tingles tingle their tune with no signs of stopping. In fact, they seem to heat up with the first little sliver of light that comes through our blinds. My cheeks warm, and I keep one eye on Luke, waiting for him to stir awake.

Perhaps he gave me a disease?

Some sort of kissing disease.

What's the name of that one you get?

Mononucleosis.

Yeah, that's what we learned about in school.

I must have that.

"Morning," Luke's morning rasp startles me from my tingles, alerting my full attention back to him. He's lying on his side, eyes turned toward me with a little sleepy smile on his lips. "How'd you sleep?"

"Ah, fine." I rustle my blanket, first tucking it tight around my waist but that feels itchy.

Or maybe I'm just itchy.

It's the mononucleosis advancing in stages. I'm going to need a doctor. It has to be, because it wouldn't be anything else. I'm so uncomfortable, I whip the blanket back down and jump out of bed. "I, ah, might run out for coffee."

"I can go if you need something." He promptly sits up straight and scratches the back of his head, as if it's helping to pull him further awake. "You can stay and get ready, and I'll go. We have to be at the airport by noon."

"You got us tickets?" I involuntarily step back, away from Luke, as looking at him makes the tingles pulse faster.

"Yeah, I told you we need to go to Vegas for the night. There is only one direct flight. With the time change and all, it's not too bad. We should be there by dinner. I got a hotel, and we can hang out and take a few photos for my dad. We fly back in the morning."

"Just like that. So easy." I grin, feeling the toothiness of my smile as I turn toward the bathroom. "In that case, I guess I'll shower and get ready."

"Perfect." He drops both feet to the floor, standing in one swift motion. "I'll run down to the dining center to grab us breakfast, and it'll be ready when you get back."

"Sure, I'll have coffee with two—"

"Two sugars and cream," he finishes my coffee request, an easy smile on his lips.

My brow furrows in pause. "How'd you know my coffee order?"

Obviously, he's been around me many times at my parents' house, and it makes sense that he just noticed. The same way you notice other random things, like when the mail lady comes or when there's paint chipping off the wall. Just normal boring things people notice all the time.

It doesn't *mean* anything.

I wait for him to brush it off, but he doesn't say anything. Instead, he smiles at me sort of rascally as he heads out the door and says, "I'll be right back."

And just like that, my mononucleosis returns.

Seriously, it's getting so dire I need a doctor, but I don't have time for a doctor because apparently, I have a plane to catch.

With Luke.

To Vegas.

To pretend to get married.

It's all so great and fabulous.

Ba ha ha.

My brows skirt to my hairline, and I beeline to the bathroom, feeling my mononucleosis swell, shooting roots into my throat. Yep, it's advancing to another stage.

It won't be long now, and I'll be fully infected.

Grabbing my throat, I gulp.

I mean, it couldn't be anything else.

A few moments later, I trip on my own foot and stumble out of the bathroom, barely catching myself as my gaze finds Luke.

Yep, reliable Luke, standing in the corner, and he's changed into jeans and another one of his insulated vests. This one is navy and matches his eyes. Not that I would notice those types of things. It's just so hard being here when I'm mononucleosising. I inch forward, fighting the urge to crawl back into bed and cover my head, avoiding him altogether.

"I got your coffee, and they actually had your favorite flavor of muffin." He motions to the bag on my bed, and I stare at it suspiciously.

"Banana chocolate chip?" The rhythmic pounding you only hear in horror movies echoes through my head as I fight the urge not to look.

"Yeah. You still like that, right?"

"S-sure." I take a wobbly step forward. "They had that at the dining center?"

"Well, no." He stuffs both hands in his pocket. He seems to be studying me, waiting for a reaction. "I had to run to the coffee shop down the road, where I knew they would have them."

My fingers practically tremble when I reach for the bag and unroll the top. Rich, earthy, dark chocolate aroma wafts from the bag, and my mouth immediately waters. I don't ask how he knew what kind of muffin I like.

My tingles return, but this time they spiral around, taking a spot in my heart, and I know better than to blame it on mononucleosis.

Somehow, in the last twenty-four hours, Luke's infected me with something so much worse than a deadly kissing disease.

It's what happens when a guy knows your coffee order and your favorite muffin without having to ask.

This is a full-blown crush.

My heart tanks, echoing all of the times I thought of him as Slobberlips, while simultaneously swelling with all the tingles that have been swarming inside me, and I can no longer deny it.

I'm smitten with Luke Slobberlips.

"I can't believe you booked us a room with a view of the Eiffel Tower." I stand in front of the window of our luxury suite at the Paris Las Vegas hotel, holding back the curtain. My lips part with awe as I take in the Vegas nightlights.

"Well, it's supposed to be a wedding weekend, right? My dad's going to want all the evidence. Speaking of which, turn toward me and smile." Luke comes up behind me, pausing a step back with his phone posed to take a photo. I flash him a playful smile—for the photo proof of course—and he adjusts the camera, taking a couple of shots.

"If it's okay, let me sneak in one of us together," he says as he slides in next to me, bringing one arm up on my lower back and the other to hold the phone away for the selfie. We grin at the camera and wait. Due to our last-minute plane tickets leaving us sitting on opposite sides of the plane, I didn't have to sit next to him on the way here, and we got zero photos together. We rode the shuttle together, but it was stuffed with other people already starting their vacation partying. We sat quietly in the back seat of the transport van, eyeing each other, as if neither one of us was sure what was happening next.

He snaps the photo and drops his phone, but the ambiance of the room is setting off a series of quakes in my chest. He got a two-bedroom suite—*for obvious reasons*—but it has an adjoined sitting room, where we are now. I'm doing my best to act like this is any casual encounter, all the while my heart is pounding against my chest.

"We need to get some food. How about that huge buffet they have here?" His eyes return to his phone, scrolling for places to eat. This whole time it seems like all he wants to do is fidget with that phone. "Or there's a *Marriage Can be Murder Dinner Show*, if you want to eat and watch a show."

"Speaking of marriage"—I turn to him— "what's the plan for that?"

"I'm glad you asked." He sweeps his gaze up at me. "I think the receipts from the trip and a few pictures will be all the proof we need, but we do need to make sure to get one photo either inside the chapel—if it's open—or standing out front."

"That makes sense." I nod, while tiny little bubbles fizzle in my gut. "Maybe we figure out where the chapel is, and then plan to grab food that way, so we aren't wasting a bunch of time running in circles."

"They have a chapel right here at our hotel, so that's no problem at all."

"This is much simpler than I thought." An easy breath flows into my chest. "Should we head down and get that over with? Then we are free to get something to eat."

"Sounds like a plan. We can just change and head down." Luke claps his hands together in front of him, before tacking on, "The hotel concierge said your dresses should be in the master bedroom closet."

"My dress*es*?" I quirk my eyebrows.

"Yeah, I had a dress rental place send over a few for you to choose from. Don't worry." He holds up an interjecting finger. "I have a tux too. Everything will look completely legit."

"Dresses." I'm still stuck on that word.

"Yeah. I hope it's okay." His words are slow, becoming measured as he takes a few steps into the adjoining master room, stopping at the closet. He opens the door, and lowers his palm, presenting a row of dresses to me. "We have to look the part. Remember, my dad's a lawyer. I didn't know what you'd like, so I had them select four of their top selling ones. You don't have to like them of course." He shifts his weight and fidgets with the hem of his shirt. "It's just for a quick photo. Thirty minutes, tops."

As my eyes rake over the dresses, my heart speeds up. I've never even tried on a wedding gown before, and here I was asked to wear one *in front of Luke.*

"Are you mad?" Luke's gaze is lasered in one me. "Did I do something wrong?"

"No," I fill in the silence. "Not wrong. When I agreed to say we got married, I didn't think we'd do anything like this. It's sort of oddly emotional to be asked to wear a wedding gown."

"You don't have to if you aren't comfortable. I'm sure plenty of people get married here in street clothes. I just wanted *our wedding* to look special, like it meant something to us."

The words *our wedding* slam into my throat, clogging it with so much emotion.

"Are you okay?" he asks after I'm quiet for a long beat.

"Yeah, I'll just change clothes." I set my gaze on the first dress. It's a sleeveless A-line silhouette, with a V-neck and a sheer lace train. *It's exquisite.* I've never seen a dress like this before, let alone worn one. I swallow and look away. There's no way I'm going to stand here getting attached to a dress. It's a mere transaction. I swallow again, stuffing down my emotion and say, "Let's do this."

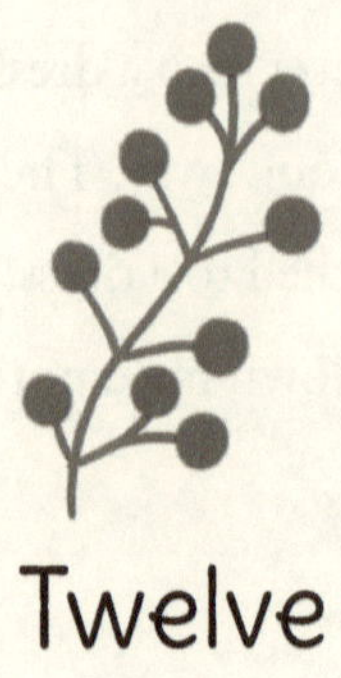

Twelve

Luke

I blink.

Somehow, I've entered an alternate universe. One where all my dreams play out before me. Noelle's standing in front of me, wearing a silk wedding gown, and her long hair hangs over her shoulder in loose boho curls. My throat twists into knots, holding back all the words I dare not actually speak.

Like how I always longed to tell her she's the single most beautiful woman I've ever laid eyes on.

Or, how when she's in the same room as me, I can't do anything but struggle not to stare at her.

Or, how I've loved her since middle school, and despite doing everything I could to make the feelings stop, they only grew stronger.

And the biggest admission of them all—*I love her.*

And if my pattern is any indication of how things will be going forward, my heart will more than likely always carry a torch for her. I've tried to tame this flame so many times, but it's so powerful. In moments like this, it burns hot in my chest, making everything about her completely irresistible.

"How do I look?" Her perfect row of top teeth pinch her bottom lip in the cutest expression of nerves.

You look like all my dreams are coming true.

"Like a masterpiece. A walking Raphael." My voice is low, concealing all the thoughts I don't add.

She walks forward, stopping in front of the full-length mirror, and her lips quickly part. "Wow, I look like a bride."

"I definitely think you play the part well." I suck back a groan, begging to come out, by tacking on, "We won't have any problems convincing my dad."

Nope, the only problem we'll have is me falling in love with you even more . . . as if that's even possible.

I fumble for my phone, holding it up. "Remember, I need proof."

"Oh, yes." She turns slightly, squaring herself with my camera and points a smile at me, and I freeze. I should be snapping the picture and getting on with this charade, but the flame in my chest nearly doubles in size, stamping out all my oxygen as I stare at her.

If this is an alternate reality, I don't ever want to leave.

My finger finds the camera button, and I regretfully press it, knowing this night is nothing more than a play.

I can't get attached.

Once again, I swallow down my emotions. "Shall we head down?"

She takes a step toward the door, but trips on her small train and stumbles forward. I immediately step into line and reach out to her, catching her palms against my chest. Her eyes hook mine, and we pause into a stillness, her warm breath wafting on me.

"Sorry." Her cheeks blush as she straightens her spine and backs away from me.

"It's okay. I didn't realize these were hazardous. Let me help." I bend over, taking a bundle of the train fabric in my hand.

"I didn't realize either." She lightly chuckles as we pace forward with me on her heels, holding the train of her dress. "I guess that's why brides have a maid of honor."

"Right." I snicker as we pass through the door, and I pull it closed behind us. "I guess now we know for *next time.*"

Next time.

It echoes in the hall, reminding me this is a dress rehearsal for someday. Every few steps she passes a glance over her shoulder back at me, and my heart skips a beat. There's no doubt these images of her in a wedding gown are being burned into my brain, and if I don't end up with some sort of long-term brain damage over this, it'll be a miracle.

We make it down the elevator with the only thing tripping being my heart.

"Do you think this is a little extreme to go to these lengths to pretend we got married?" Noelle's gaze pins on me as we slowly shuffle toward the chapel. In front of a wide-open door, a magnolia flower arch welcomes us into the empty chapel.

"One thing about me," I breathe out, not taking my eyes off the long aisle and rows of seats in front of us. "When I commit to something, I do it big."

"I guess." She inches forward, slowing her steps even more before passing a wavering glance over her shoulder at me. "We don't need to go *inside* the chapel, right? I think if we take a photo from here with it in the background, it sells the narrative enough."

Hating to make her uncomfortable, I nod reassuringly as I reach in my suit jacket pocket for my phone. "This is fine." Just as I'm positioning my phone in the perfect selfies center, we are interrupted by a slicing voice.

"Next!" My gaze follows the voice to a stout man wearing what looks like a baby-blue vintage tux, with a berry red and pine needle corsage pinned to the lapel, and he's waving us inside the chapel. "Next couple, please."

"Sorry, we don't mean to block your chapel. We're just taking a photo." I reach behind Noelle, hooking my hand on her waist and scooch us both over to the far wall out of the doorway.

"Let's keep the line moving. You're next." He bobbles his head our way, aggressively waving us inside.

Noelle's nervous giggle bubbles out, and she tosses a look back at him. "We're not getting married."

"You can't fool me." The man pins a closed fist on his hip. "I've seen cold feet before. In fact, it happens at least once a day. Trust me, it's pretty painless. You walk up the aisle, say your vows, and the whole thing is done in ten minutes. Unless you want to pay for the premium package. We can do a half hour ceremony where you get a full sermon and scriptures."

"We actually only want a photo and no ceremony." I step forward, holding my phone out to him. "How much will it cost to take our photo in front of the altar?"

He pauses for a beat, his gaze bouncing from me to Noelle before he directs a wink toward Noelle. "Photos are free as long as you make it snappy and stop holding up the line."

"Great," I gush out. "We really appreciate this."

"No problem. Come with me, and I'll snap it for you." He waves us forward, this time waddling down the aisle in front of us. Once he gets to the front, he stops and reaches for my phone, holding it up while he waits for us to position ourselves standing next to each other. "So, getting back at an ex-lover or trying to secure an inheritance?"

I pass a shy glance to Noelle, but don't expound on his question. "Why would you think that?"

"I've ran this chapel for a decade, and trust me, there's always a reason people need a picture at the altar with no vows." He twirls his index finger in a circle, like he's rushing us along. "All right, let's get it right the first time so I can get on with my day. Big smiles."

I pull Noelle to my side, holding her close to me in a traditional wedding church pose, and I think I smile. It's hard to tell as her nearness has made my entire body go numb. After a fast moment, the man hands back my phone. "There you go. Remember photos are free, but tips are extra."

"Oh." My head jerks back, and I immediately pat my coat pocket for my wallet. "Of course. Is a twenty okay?" I fan through my cash as I never carry much on me.

"Fifty is better, and for a hundred, I can accidentally slip you a frame-quality chapel certificate. You can fill it out to make it look like you had a real ceremony."

"Ah, I might need to get some cash." I slip the twenty back in my wallet and scan the room for a cashier.

"There's a time machine right outside the casino." He starts to pace back down the aisle, clearly ushering us out.

"Time machine?" I echo, angling my gaze at him as I'm starting to wonder if there's something a little off about him.

"Yes, ATM, Actual Time Machine," he calls back over his shoulder. "We're in Vegas. Time is money, and you're wasting mine now."

"S-Sorry," I stutter, reaching for Noelle's hand as I propel her back out of the chapel. "I'll grab the cash and be right back."

"Very well." He holds up a finger, waving us to the side while jutting his chin out to call over the crowd, "Next!"

Noelle and I dart around the corner, falling into each other over fits of giggles before we finally stop and burst out laughing. "Time machine," I gasp, still wondering what was up with that man.

"What was that?" She takes the words out of my mouth, as she holds her stomach while waves of giggles pour out.

"I guess he's seen his fair share of fake weddings down here, and he clearly has a well-run ship."

"I guess." The last of her giggles die out, and she points to the ATM in the corner, exactly where that guy said it would be. "There's the ah, *time* machine."

Giggles bubble out of both our lips as we move in unison to the ATM. Right as I push my debit card into the slot, a barmaid comes up to Noelle and hands her a champagne flute. "Free glass for the bride."

"Oh," Noelle rushes, "I'm not actually a—" The server winks and walks off, and Noelle stares at the glass before raising an eyebrow toward me. "I guess we fooled her."

I grab my cash out of the machine and grin, as this night has just begun, and it's already so strange. "Not actually free if you think about it." I fan my cash in front of her face. "Remember, tips are extra."

Her lips spread into a full smile as she laughs from deep in her belly. That might be my favorite expression of hers. The full belly laugh, especially when I cause it. I join in her laughter, not because I'm feeling silly, but because I can't stand to not share in her joy. When the laughter quiets, I hold up the cash again. "All right, let's pay off shortie, before he reports our scandal to the *National Enquirer*, and then we can find some place to eat. Does that sound like a plan?"

"It sounds like the perfect plan." Noelle smiles sweetly at me, before hooking her arm in mine like a real bride, and we stroll back through the casino. It takes about another five steps before we literally run into someone else.

A wide man in a Santa suit is bent over with his head stuck in the open end of a giant cloth sack.

"Whoops." Noelle bounces a step back. "I'm so sorry. Excuse me."

Santa pulls his head out of his sack and straightens up. Upon seeing our wedding attire his grin fills in. "Ah, what do we have here? Newlyweds?"

"Yes, ah, Santa." Noelle's gaze bounces from the guy to me. "Just got married."

"Congratulations." He puts his arm into his sack and digs around, all the while his gaze doesn't leave Noelle. "Let me see what I have for you."

"Oh, no need for presents." She tries to wave him off.

"Nonsense, tell me what your Christmas wish is?" He offers her a grand gesture forward with his free hand.

"Ah, truthfully"—she pulls up her brow and lowers her tone—"I need some extra money. Not a new job, because I love my job, but some sort of side hustle that isn't soul crushing."

He winks at her and hands over a candy cane from his sack, then turns to me. "And you, sir? What would you like this year?"

I smash my lips together, as I gaze back at Noelle. There isn't a single thing in the world I could ask for more than this moment. "I ah, have everything I need this year. Maybe take my wish to double down on her wish, if you can."

Santa produces another candy cane and passes it to me. Instead of saying Merry Christmas, or something normal, he says, "I already know. Christmas is the season of miracles." He pats me on the forearm and walks off without another word.

"That was odd." I toss a glance over my shoulder, and he's gone. I didn't catch what direction he went. He just blended in with the crowd. Odd for a fat guy in a bright red suit to blend in . . .

"That was sweet of you to give me your wish." Noelle's voice pulls my gaze to her, and I take a deep swallow.

"Of course." I downplay my gesture, teasing the newlywed theme. "Now that we're married, I want all of your dreams to come true too."

Her lips roll in for a moment. "It's getting late. Let's go pay off shortie."

"Right." My head springs back, and I remember what we were doing before we ran into Santa. "Let's head out this way." I take a step forward, all the while my heart patters against my chest, soaking up the way it feels to have Noelle on my arm as my bride.

I'm clearly going to die over this.

Thirteen

Noelle

We playfully clasp our hands together, acting the part of newly-weds as we stroll down the Vegas Strip. I don't even feel odd holding his hand, as it's actually comfortable, and we quickly learned to milk the wedding attire. In addition to the champagne, I've also gotten two coupons for a free dinner and a half-off code to the hotel spa. As a broke girl, who was nearly homeless, I'm going to keep this act up to see what else I can get.

It's a tad chilly but not nearly as cold as Vermont this time of year. The sun's gone down, and the lights are radiating with abundant energy, fueling excitement to bud in my chest. I'm not a gambler, but you don't need to be one to enjoy walking around out here.

Plus, Luke's subconsciously—or maybe on purpose—pulling me to his side, like I'm his actual bride. Not only is it doing everything to keep me physically warm, but it's also bringing all these fizzy little sparks to ignite in my chest. I'd have to be a real Scrooge to not feel the romance in the air as we stroll along in our wedding garments with people cheering and congratulating us wherever we walk.

"Where would you like to eat?" Luke's steel-cut jaw bends toward me, and it's all I can do to not stare at the perfect angle. Having avoided looking at his lips for the last ten years, I completely missed out on that nearly right-angle gift on his face.

"How about one of those giant hot dogs from that stand?" I nod toward the place right up the block. There's a small line wrapped outside of it, but it seems to be moving fairly fast.

"You're wearing a wedding dress, and you want to eat a hot dog?"

"The dress doesn't turn me into a vegan, if that's what you're thinking." I laugh, a hearty sound. "I've always been one of those girls who needs to eat. Salads don't do a thing for me."

"Right." He stops in the back of the hotdog line, standing with enough room in front of him for me to cut in line before him, and I slide in. "I wasn't implying you shouldn't eat. I thought you'd want something a bit fancier. I could get you a steak or something. Since it's our faux wedding and all."

"Nah, then we have to go inside, and I sort of love it out here."

We reach the front of the line, and Luke flashes a look at me, seeking approval. "Two hotdogs with all the toppings?"

"Everything." I nod, tacking on, "And napkins."

The guy working the stand punches in our orders and takes Luke's card without saying anything. We step to the side as he hands us two heavily decorated hot dogs over his cart. "Do they have bibs?" I eye the sauces piled high, my mouth already watering.

"Too late now." Luke's lips slide into a daring smile. "We're fully committed. Do you want to race?"

"Race to see how fast we can eat?" I scoff, as that sounds like a terrible idea. I'll more than likely get ill, but he doesn't know how competitive I am. If there's one sport I'm good at, it's eating. "I don't know about that." I nibble off the end of my hotdog, fully intending to get a cheating head start, and swallow my first bite before I rush to say, "Ready, set, eat!" I'm into my second bite, and his brows are pinned all the way to his hairline.

"Hey, you cheated!"

The longer he talks, the further he gets behind, and I shove another bite in and chew. He's caught on now, breaking off a giant bite alongside me, and we take turns biting and chewing until I take my last bite, and swallow it down, announcing with two fists in the air, "You lose!"

He's laughing and choking on his bite. "I guess if you want to be a cheater."

"Nope, not a cheater; just a proactive starter."

Shaking his head, his smile wins his expression. "Noelle, you're a poor winner."

"There's no such thing as a poor winner. Only the best winner and that's me." I dab the corners of my mouth with my napkin, feeling my stomach expand with each new breath. "Ah, man." I place a hand on the center of my gut. "That might have been a bad idea."

His smirk shows no empathy. "That's what you get for being a cheater—"

"Winner," I correct him, even inserting a point-making finger in the air as I laugh before grabbing at my stomach again to wince. "Man, not a good idea. I might need to lie down."

"We can head back." He glances over his shoulder toward our hotel. "We got our wedding photos and food. We did what we set out to do."

"Are you sure?" I'm partially leaning now, as my stomach is twisting into reflux bubbles.

"It's fine." He motions for us to start walking, and I slide my foot forward. "We have an early flight to catch anyway."

"Sorry for ruining our wedding night." I wobble as best as I can. "Note to self, on the real one, don't race you to eat a hotdog."

"Right, because next time you'll lose." He competitively snickers, a gleam sparking out the corner of his eye.

"Never," I fake-growl, and we burst out into a fit of cackling all the way back to the hotel.

Outside the hotel, the Eiffel Tower is lit up, sparkling in Christmas colors of green and red and gold. It's so stunning, I gasp. "Wow, I've never seen anything like it."

"Imagine what the real one looks like." Luke pauses next to me, but he seems to be watching me more than the tower.

"I guess that's goals for the next wedding," I tease, trying to keep the mood light, but when my gaze shifts back to Luke, he's staring at me with a serious expression in his eyes. "What?"

"I think we should get a picture of us dancing on our wedding night." He retrieves his phone from his pocket, and turns to the woman standing closest to him, saying, "Do you mind taking our photo? It's our wedding day."

"Of course." She takes the phone and immediately holds it up, and I'm not going to be rude to tell her we don't actually need this photo.

Luke extends his hand, and I place my palm in his. At the same time, we each take a step closer, making the gap between us pretty much nonexistent. He leads me in a slow circle, and people around us watch, awing about how our wedding night is so gorgeous. The lady takes the photo and slides Luke's phone back to him. He receives the phone, slipping it in his pocket, but he doesn't let go of me. If anything, his hold becomes stronger, his fingers spread over my lower back.

He's quiet.

His tender gaze holds power. One that has somehow found a way to slice right through my chest, grounding in a place that nobody had ever taken root in before.

This Eiffel Tower is a fake.

This wedding was fake.

Our marriage is fake.

This dance started out fake, but nothing about this moment feels fake.

Heat flares under my cheeks, and I struggle not to lean closer. I'm clearly delusional, but my mind is getting confused with all the pretending, and frankly I don't want to pretend.

I can't pretend.

My heart is pumped so full of all the swoony feelings as Luke guides me around, under the fake Eiffel Tower, and I realize I don't care if it's all fake. I still love every moment of it.

"There." Luke's deep declaration breaks through my thoughts as he halts our steps. "I think we did all the things. Are you ready to go back?"

No.

I'm not ready to go back to the hotel.

My thoughts rewind over this whole night, none of these events were my idea. Luke took care of all the details. I didn't have to worry about anything, and even though it's fake, it meant something.

Not to mention the whole reason behind it—to help me find an affordable house. How I got so lucky to find someone like Luke is beyond me. And even though it's fake, a massive swarm of butterflies flows into my chest, and he needs to know how much I appreciate all of this.

"Is something wrong?" His eyes lock on mine, as if silently challenging me.

I shake my head back and forth, with his gaze still pinned on me, and I place my hand on his forearm to steady myself. I lean up on my toes and plant a kiss on his cheek. As I pull away, I begin to murmur, "Thank you for—"

Before I have a chance to drop all the way to my flat feet, his hand finds my chin, locking it in place, while his other hand wraps around my back, sweeping me right against his chest, and his lips come crashing back down to find mine.

Quite literally sweeping me into a kiss that takes me off my feet as I lean back into his arm.

Soft at first, his tenderness puts me at ease, and I breathe into his kiss, as my heart unwinds with each unfolding.

Maybe it's Vegas.

Maybe it's the dress. I mean, I do look like a princess.

I have an impossible time not believing whatever it is, is not real, and I'm breathless by the time I pull away. Our gazes instantly collide, finding their way back to each other, and there is something new between us now.

"Sorry, I just felt like a bride as stunning as you needed to be properly kissed." His expression isn't sorry. I'm speechless as he reaches for my hand, and I willingly give it to him, and we link our fingers together.

My heart is thrumming hard against my chest as we walk back to our room, where he promptly says goodnight before heading into his room, leaving me to ponder.

At least for me, I'm not faking anything any more.

Is he?

Fourteen

Luke

I lie in bed, staring at the ceiling with my eyes in the shape of hearts. I willed the sleep away because I was afraid if I fall asleep, I'll wake up back in my old reality. I'm enjoying this new reality way too much.

I'll remember tonight for the rest of my life. Even when it implodes my heart into literally ashes to let Noelle move on with her life, it will have been worth it.

But who is to say it has to be over?

That's the thought I cling to the hardest when I groggily crawl out of bed the next morning. Shuffling in the dark, I try my hardest to stay quiet to not wake Noelle, but I need to pack and get ready for the airport.

When I open my door to enter our shared sitting room, Noelle is sitting on the couch, staring at her phone, with the cord plugged in. My eyes narrow, as that looks like my phone charger, but I distinctly remember plugging my phone in before I went to bed.

I cut a glance at my phone sitting on the coffee table, not plugged in. "Are you using my phone charger?" I step forward, glaring at that thing attached to her phone. That is in fact my charger. Scooping up my phone, I noticed it is only half charged, and I tilt my head toward her.

"Oh, I'm sorry. I can't find my charger, and my phone was all the way dead. Since yours had some charge, I thought it would be okay." She pulls the plug out of her phone, reaching the end to me. "You can have it back."

I blow out a calming breath, checking the time. I want it fully charged for the long day of travel, but it's not a big deal. It's just a phone. A small sacrifice to make for the love of my life. "We need to leave for the airport in the next fifteen minutes, so I won't have time to charge it."

"I'm sorry." She pins a toothy expression on her face.

"*It's fine.*" I put my phone into battery saving mode before I tuck it in my vest pocket. "Are you ready?"

"Yeah, I am." She stands and grabs her purse while stowing her *fully charged* phone inside. "Next time, I'll remember to bring my own charger," she adds as she pulls the end out of the wall plug and hands it to me.

Maybe it's my lack of sleep that is triggering me, but I force a smile toward her. Then I focus on all the positive feelings from last night, and it doesn't take long for my forced smile to turn into a real one.

Today, I fly back from Vegas with my "wife," and we get our new home.

What could be better than that?

On the airplane, we sit next to each other, sharing a middle and window seat at the very back of the plane. I'm so excited to be this close to her for a long trip. Hopefully, we can snuggle and rekindle some of those sparks we had last night. I eye the window longingly before stepping back out of the way to make room for Noelle to pass. "Why don't you take the window seat?"

"Are you sure?" She raises a brow toward me, but she's already beelining toward the coveted seat. "It's my favorite spot."

"Yeah." I sandwich myself in the narrow seat aisle, as something already feels off about this row. It's clearly way smaller than the other rows, and I duck under the overhead compartment to land on my middle seat.

If taking the middle seat on a plane isn't love, then I'm not sure what is.

It's all going to be worth it when Noelle sees how much I care about her, and I grit my teeth together and force a positive tone. "I actually look forward to sitting next to *complete strangers* so I can meet new people."

"Not me." Noelle blows out a sigh as she relaxes her head back and shimmies her arm onto our shared armrest. Eight out of eight dentists would agree that since I gave her the window seat, the shared armrest should be mine, but I pause and do the most gentlemanly thing I can muster. I hike a brow, waiting for her to offer the armrest. My gentlemanly ways go unnoticed because her eyes are closed. I resign to hijacking the other armrest before my neighbor moves in.

"Excuse me, sir." A woman with a baby on her hip slides in, claiming the seat in one big motion. "Do you mind holding my son while I get his bottle ready?"

The baby in question stares at me with wide eyes, drool slathered over the entire southern hemisphere of his face. "Ah, sure." I reach out, hooking a hand below each of the kid's armpits. When I get a whiff of his spit-up breath, I secure him a proper arm length away from my nose. "Cute little feller," I mumble, trying to sound like holding a baby during a plane ride is *not* my worst nightmare.

"Thanks." She drops an oversized carry-on bag onto the floor, and jabs her foot on it, trying to push it under the seat in front of her with no luck. She gives up, and sits back, holding a bottle in her lap, and proceeds to squeeze the air out of a little sack in the slowest setting. The kid has now noticed that I'm not his mama, and his real mama has a bottle of his milk. Something is drastically wrong with his facial expression, and he drops his bottom lip wide open and wails out a deafening cry for help.

I thrust the baby toward his mother, dangling him over her lap, but she's still squeezing the air out of the sack.

She must be deaf.

It's the only way she can function with that noise. People are looking at me now, and I imagine they think it's my baby, and I'm disturbing the plane. "It's okay, little guy," I whisper, but it's not like anyone can hear anything over his wails. The kid has the lungs of a grizzly bear. It's a grizzlybaby. I reposition him, pulling him to my chest, anchoring an arm under his bum, and try to pat his back like I've seen people do in the movies.

I know nothing about babies.

Clearly, it doesn't work, and the baby screams harder, and I growl out to the mom, "Are you done with that bottle yet?"

"Oh yes." She has a smooth Southern accent, as if this is a Sunday stroll. "Sorry, he has terrible reflux. If I leave one air bubble, he will vomit it right back up. I figured since you have to sit next to him, you wouldn't want that." She laughs at her own joke, but I don't even fake a grin, as sitting next to a vomiting-grizzly-bear baby on a nonstop flight is not on my Bingo card—ever.

On any planet.

Finally, she takes the baby back, cradling him into her loving arms to feed him but not before propping that arm on *my armrest.* Horror alarms sound as she takes the only other armrest that I have access to.

I'm stuck sitting like a stiff board, because I don't want to risk offending either of these women.

This is just great.

Now that my hands are free, my gaze skirts back to Noelle, and her eyes are still closed. She slept through this whole thing, all the while still hogging the armrest! Her breath is heavy and relaxed like she's having the best sleep of her life.

How is this fair?

We never had these problems before we were married.

First my phone charger, and then screaming hungry babies that she sleeps through.

Aren't I supposed to at least have a honeymoon before the babies come?

It's like as soon as our vows were said, all these problems came.

What is next?

Oh, no, I wasn't asking for something else!

The grizzlybaby cackles, spitting out the nipple of his bottle, and proceeds to cough. It all happens in slow motion as the mother lifts him up and presses him to her shoulder for a nice hearty burp.

An extra juicy burp that lands on my arm.

Yep, I never knew burps had actual mass to them, but they do.

I see it.

It's chunky and fizzing with all the grossness I never imagined possible. I bite back a massive gurgle in my throat.

My gaze slides back to Noelle.

She missed it all again.

She's sleeping like Sleeping Beauty, just as beautiful as ever.

Her beauty erases my grumps, immediately.

It's all going to be worth it.

I pull my brain back to focus on only positive things.

It's just one plane ride, and then it's off to endless snuggles on the couch watching TV together, and late-night dinners of our favorite takeout and a bottle of wine, last-minute weekend getaways, and never-ending smiles.

I just need to survive this plane ride.

Fifteen

Noelle

My eyes flutter open as the plane bounces onto the tarmac to land, and immediately I see Luke—*with a baby!*

I double blink. Yes, there's a real baby propped against his shoulder, and it appears they know each other.

I lightly squeeze his forearm, expecting him to turn to me and smile. Instead, his whole body seems to seize in tension as his head rotates to me, and he nearly pants, "You awake finally?"

Inhaling, I bend backward, rolling my back into a decent stretch. My neck is a little cramped from sleeping against the window, but all in all, I had the best flight. Such a peaceful rest, and this whole weekend has been nothing but dreamy. I bat my lashes at him, ready to banter. "I had the best dreams."

"Oh, yeah?" His tone is terse, and he's barely looking at me, except for an almost-angered side-eye every few seconds. "That's nice. We landed, which means you slept for *seven hours*."

"I had major catching up on sleep to do." I blink, doing the math. "If I count what I slept last night, that's like fifteen hours of sleep." I giggle, as clearly this whole marriage thing is working out in my favor. I'm giddy knowing we are getting a new house this week. I don't have to look for a new job, and I get to keep Buttercup. All that good news would be enough to send me into a huge spiral of relief. Add that to all the tingles Luke's been sending my way, and I'm on cloud one hundred and nine. "If I would have known how much fun yesterday would be, I would have insisted we do this marriage thing years ago," I tease, giving Luke a playful wink, but he only returns a stony glare. "Where did you say that baby came from?" I ask after he never replies.

People are standing now, filing into the aisle as passengers depart the plane. The baby coos over Luke's shoulder, and I melt. It's the cutest thing I've ever seen. "This baby?" Luke grumbles, barely looking at the infant, but it's clear the baby is smitten with him, making big wide-mouth smiles at him.

"Yeah." My lips curl into a playful smile, and I lean forward to coo back at the baby. "He's so cute."

"It's so funny you should ask." Luke shifts the baby, moving him to the opposite shoulder—farther away from me—as he stands, claiming a spot in the center aisle. "You see, this baby sat down next to me *seven hours* ago. He's flying with his single mother, and apparently, she got some stomach bug, oh, like a whole hour and sixteen minutes ago, and fled to the back bathroom, leaving a trail of vomit, but not before she gave him to me."

"Oh no." My eyes find the back of the plane. There's a woman sitting in one of the flight attendant's seats, strapped in and her face is deep into a barf bag. I've never seen an airline allow anyone to remain out of their seat during landing, but I guess her being there was a last-ditch effort. "She didn't even make it back to her seat for landing." I shake my head. "That poor woman."

"Right. That poor woman." He slides a foot down the aisle, heading toward the back of the plane. "But hey, you got fifteen hours of sleep, so we're cool."

I freeze as Luke proceeds to walk the baby back to reunite with his mom, and I'm getting the sinking feeling that he's mad at me for something, which is absurd. He was so happy yesterday, and this whole day feels off.

He hands over the baby. A few minutes later he's back beside our row, but the line in front of us has cleared. We're basically the last few passengers on the plane. "We can leave now," Luke mutters as he collects his backpack from the overhead bin, waiting for me to get out of the row.

I gather my purse and my bag and step in front of him. "So, are we headed to the dorm, or do we get our house right away?" I know the answer, but I'm over-the-moon excited to see what this place looks like and start our new life *together*.

That word zings in my gut like the sweetest Hershey's Kiss, making everything so much better. Nobody could convince me that this marriage situation would ever make me want to curl my toes, but I'm excited to see where this goes. After a kiss like we shared last night, at this point, I'm believing anything is possible.

"Dorm." His one-word answer tips me off again that something might be wrong with him.

"Okay." I'm at the plane exit now, and step onto the jet bridge, heading inside the terminal. "Do you think we should at least call your parents to tip them off that we have a surprise? I'm thinking if we were truly newlyweds, we wouldn't wait to tell people, especially our parents."

"I can't call them because my phone is dead." The amount of disgruntled inflection grumbling in his voice surprises me. I don't ever remember Luke being a grump before.

"Well, here." I reach into my purse, and grab my phone wrapped in a pink-glitter case. "Use mine." I turn it on, swipe my password to unlock it, and hand it to him.

"Whoa. What." His eyes sweep over my notifications blowing up my phone as it loads, and his eyes swell. "You have four missed calls from Don, and a text message. Who is this Don guy?"

I peer at my phone, finding it rather odd Don called me that much. "What did the message say? Is Buttercup okay?"

"I don't know anything about Buttercup." He passes my phone back, and I open my text message while he blurts out, "But I don't think some Don guy should be messaging you that much now that we're married. I'm not going to be at home making sourdough while you're sending pics to some dude."

First of all, we aren't really married, and second, what is his problem? He's never been grumpy before, and I'm stunned. We stride together down the corridor, bypassing the luggage claim. Not that I have to explain myself, but the silence is getting stale, and I offer, "Don is my boss, and nobody is messaging me."

His perfect jaw muscles twitch, but he doesn't refute my explanation. To lighten the mood, I tack on, "Besides, I doubt you can make sourdough."

"Is that a challenge?" One of his brow spikes above the other.

"You have got to be kidding." My lips are curling into a teasing smile. "You're telling me you know how to make sourdough bread?"

"I'm not as surface level as you think." His lips finally bend to a tiny coy smile. "I have many hidden talents. You just never took the time to get to know more before."

"Is being a travel grump one of these hidden talents?" I can't help but take a dig at him. "Because I'm not sure I want to know any more of them."

"I'm not a travel grump."

"Oh no." I pretend to be shocked. "Something happened to you today. I've never seen you so crabby." We reach the exit and pass through the sliding glass door together, but Luke seems to be shedding another layer of whatever funk he was in, and his lips bend even more. "We had a great day yesterday," I explain, "but clearly sleeping in that hotel made you wake up on the wrong side of the bed or something, because you've been a grump all day."

"How would you know what kind of mood I've been in. You slept all day!" Now he finally chuckles and slowly nods. "Okay, maybe you're right. I didn't sleep the best, and I don't love long plane rides. Maybe I am a travel grump. Is that so bad?"

"I'll have to see. I need to try this sourdough bread to see if that can offset the horridness of your travel flaws, or I'll be giving you this ring right back."

One side of his lips curls higher, as he catches my gaze right as we find his car. "So, you said we had a great day yesterday."

"Yeah, I had a nice time." I blink, suddenly feeling self-conscious. "Why?"

"Just checking to make sure I heard that right." He opens my car door, and I slide in, right as he adds, "Because I had the best day."

When he closes the door, my lips seal into a smirk.

Luke gets in his side of the car and immediately puts his phone in the charging station. "All right, Noelle." He starts the car and backs out of his spot. "Fake-marriage mission accomplished. Now when my phone is *charged*, I'll call my dad. We should have our new house in no time."

I lean back in my seat and start to rest my eyes, but Luke shakes my shoulder and goes on defense. "Oh no, you don't go to sleep! You do not get to go back to sleep." His words sputter out with so much angry spit, a drop lands on my face.

"I wasn't going to sleep." I wipe my cheek with my sleeve, as this interaction is bringing back Slobberlips vibes, and I pace myself to prevent my coughs. "Man." I sigh heavily, giving him a side-eye. "You have dual personalities. Am I even going to be safe to move in with you?"

He's quiet for the longest beat, making my heart pump hard, as I start to wonder what I really got myself into.

"I have no idea what to expect," he says, slowly., "But I think it's going to be surprising to us both."

I bite my lip, my gut twisting.

This whole trip was not what I expected. Everything from our wedding photos—that were quite fun—to finding out Luke is a travel grump. It's one extreme to the next. It's too late to back out now. We are about to start spending a lot more time together but now I'm hoping this house is huge, because this could be worse than I had thought.

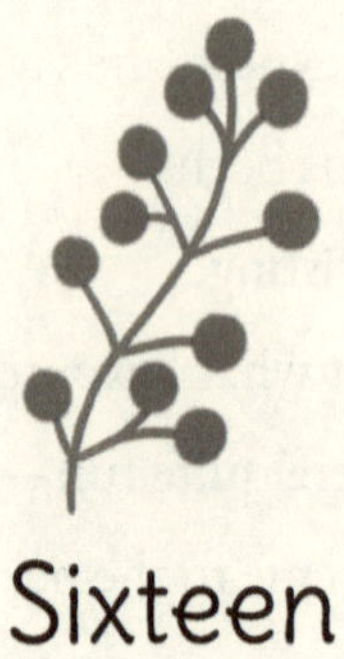

Sixteen

Luke

My fingers literally cannot straighten. They tremble with jitters as I clench the steering wheel, hooking a left into the Mapleton stables to meet Noelle. Boston flew home for the holiday, so I have my car for a few weeks.

It's Monday.

The day after we returned from our "elopement." Noelle got up early for work, barely talking to me. Turns out, she's not a Monday morning person, but that's cool. I kept my distance and slipped out the door to head to class, and when that was done, I visited my d ad.

Dad claims he had a hunch I was coming. As soon as Noelle and I had left their house the other day, he filled out the papers to claim

Grandma's house from her trust. He didn't even ask questions. I showed him the photo of Noelle and me in the chapel, and the "official" certificate. He patted my back and gave me the key. His handshake came with a stern warning that my mother was going to need more of an explanation, and more than likely she'd want to plan a church wedding and reception for us. I didn't know what to say about that. I hate to upset my mother, and I can see how she would have felt left out, but I held my stance of blaming the lack of ceremony on final exams this week and said maybe this summer.

Dad said the timing worked out perfectly with this being finals week at school. I can move out of the dorm, and he won't have to pay for spring semester housing. He seemed pretty pleased about that.

And here I am, waiting for Noelle to get off work, with a key to our new home and a secret sourdough cookbook I've stashed in my trunk because I can't let anything go. I'm going to prove to her I can make sourdough. It can't really be that hard, and I might even be so good at it, that I'll, I'll...open a sourdough bakery.

It's not extreme at all.

It could happen.

Because I'm that stubborn.

After four songs on the radio, Noelle passes through the gate, locking it behind her. Her long hair is parted on the side, bringing her hair over her shoulder. She's wearing jeans and a heavy coat as the air is getting crisper every day, but her smile is warm when she spots me. "Hey, you. What are you doing here?"

I roll down my window, leaning over to better see her walk up from behind. "I got the keys to the house, and I packed up our bags. We can go now if you want."

"Are you serious?" Her lips bend brilliantly, and her petite fingers clench into excited fists that she pumps into the air in a celebratory manner. "Yes, let's go."

I nod toward her truck across the yard. "Why don't you follow me, so we don't have to come back for your vehicle."

"Deal," she calls out, already en route, and I watch in the rearview mirror as she climbs into her truck.

My stomach twists into a nervous knot, all while my heart thrums out little, tiny hearts that float out in her direction. I'm a wreck as I back my car out, leading her down the road to *our* new home.

It's a short drive past the stables and up into the wooded hills. I've memorized this road, but I take the curves slowly to allow her time to adjust to the twists and turns. My mind is much faster, already planning all the memories we are about to make. I can't wait to show her all the things that make this house so special. I hope she likes sledding and warm chats by the fireplace.

It's supposed to snow this weekend, which means this move is just in time for the perfect cup of hot cocoa. If everything goes well, maybe another romantic moment and more kissing.

A movie of Christmas-card-cute scenes plays out in my head as I envision all the fun we are about to have in our new home. I pull into the clearing, stopping short of the house, and kill the engine. Noelle parks beside me and hops out of her truck, her eyes brimming wide as she marvels at the chateau.

I can't blame her. I still feel like that, and I have almost every inch of this place embedded into my brain.

My great-great grandparents came from France, hence why they couldn't ever just call this place a home. They were fancy and called it a chateau. They were never royalty, but that didn't stop them from enjoying architecture perfectly molded to fit the countryside. This house had been their *accidental* hunting lodge. It was built in the late 1800s, at which time when they settled here, they knew nothing about the climate and were wrongly under the impression the climate was much like the Mediterranean. They hired builders to produce a lodge to fit the homes perfectly for that climate. Six months later, a twenty-four-room house sprawled out on their one-hundred-and-twenty-acre plot in the hills.

With one big surprise looming.

It snowed a lot in Vermont, and their house wasn't insulated for this kind of weather. Rather than spend the money to basically start over, they used it as a summer hunting lodge. Over the years, my grandparents and my parents added a few modern upgrades. Indoor plumbing and removal of the lead paint being the first to happen, but it does still feel primitive now that I look around.

The porch is as wide as the house, wrapping all the way around it. Maybe that's why I love this house, because you can stand in any location on the porch and get a perfect view of the mountains.

The windows don't even have screens, as that wasn't a thing back then. Yet it docsn't hurt the aesthetic of the house—at least not in my humble opinion. As a kid, I saw this primitive place as an adventure, but now I'm biting my lip, hoping I didn't oversell it to Noelle.

It's definitely big, the size of a small hotel.

And it's secluded, the only view in every direction is wooded hills.

It's free. She has to love that.

Best of all, it's ours.

"Well." I inhale the fresh pine-scented air. "We're home. What do you say we go inside? We can look around and make a shopping list."

Out of instinct, I extend my hand to her. Her gaze bounces to my eyes before a smile breaks on her lips as she slips her hand in mine, and we walk in unison.

My heart can't contain all this fullness, and it overflows, spiraling out to my extremities, making my smile wider and my steps more energetic. I struggle to keep my eyes off her, with one worrisome thought in the back of my head.

I hope this doesn't disappoint her.

Or worse, I disappoint her.

I swallow down my fear, my stomach twisting with this crazy new indigestion, and I unlock the front door. It opens with ease, and I steal a glance at Noelle as we both step forward. Rather than look around, my gaze pins to her. It's hard to explain, but I'm sharing my favorite place on earth with Noelle, and there's a vulnerability that feels like it cracks my chest wide open. Her eyes pass the dull wood floors to land on the sparsely furnished living room with only a sheet-covered sofa. "I never said it was luxury or anything, but remember it's free, and Buttercup can stay too."

She blinks as she walks forward, the floor creaking. "I imagined it to be Victorian, but this is cozy. Do the lights work?"

"I called the power company, so they should. They aren't original to the house, as that was all added. If they need work, I can call an electrician."

"It's perfect." She breathes a sigh of relief as she turns back to me. "I appreciate it very much." She runs a hand over the back of the sheet-covered sofa. "All it needs is a good scrubbing. Don't you think?"

"Ah, yeah." I scratch the back of my head, studying the inflections in her voice, hoping she is being truthful. I don't hear any doubts braided into her words. "The lady of the house suite is on this main floor right off this room, but if you don't want that, there's twenty other rooms upstairs to pick from. However, there is no central heat or anything, and those rooms are the coldest in winter."

"This room over here?" Her finger juts to the door tucked in the corner.

"Yeah, it has its own fireplace, so you'll be warm. Why don't you go ahead and look around and see what you need? We still have time to run to town before it snows."

She walks forward, disappearing inside the room, and calls out, "It looks great. Maybe just lots of cleaning spray—" Her calm voice drops off, and it's immediately replaced with a shrill squeal. "And bug spray!"

I don't even manage to blink, and she is back by my side, cowering close behind me. "Spider," she pants out, her eyes fix on me as if she expects me to go play hero in there. I'm not scared of spiders. This house is in the country, and I've found plenty of country things over the years, but I hadn't realized this might be an issue for her. "It's on the wall, right above the bed."

"It's fine." I pace forward, unscathed, pulling my shoe off after I cross the threshold into her room. There he is. He's nothing more than a *big* old barn spider, and I smack my shoe against the wall to flatten him. "Got him," I yell back, as I watch the bug goo smear on the wall. "Yep, we need to grab lots of cleaning supplies," I tack on, but I'm smiling when I reemerge from the bedroom.

Noelle is beaming back at me as if I just saved the planet. "Thank you so much," she gushes, but she doesn't take any steps into the bedroom.

"I'll, ah, grab bug spray from town, and then I'll make sure to inspect your room when we get back," I reassure her. "Don't worry. We'll get them all taken care of, and you can rest peacefully."

Her chest falls with a heavy sigh as she slides her gaze from the room back to me. "You're the best, Luke."

Her words sting my heart in the greatest way. I lower my gaze to the wood floor and fight a beaming smile. "I just want the best for you, and I'm glad you are here."

"I'm glad I'm here too." She smiles sweetly, "But I'll be happier when I know the spiders are gone."

"Right." I straighten my posture and scan the room. Everything is move-in ready, except for needing a deep clean. "I'll run my bag upstairs to claim a room, and then we should be able to head out to get some groceries, cleaning stuff, and bug spray. Does that sound like a plan?"

"Yeah, I'll just wait right here." Her shoulders cinch together as her gaze wafts around the floorboards, scanning for more spiders.

"We'll be fine." I slide a foot in front of the other before calling back, "I can handle the spiders."

Spiders are the easy part. Not sure I can handle what this woman does to my heart.

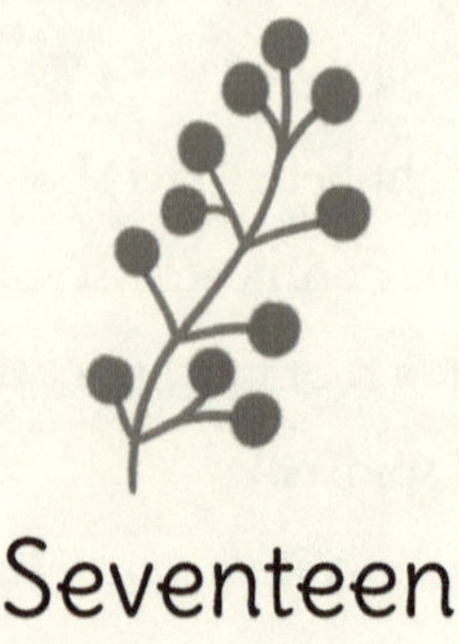

Seventeen

Noelle

"Wait until you try my sourdough." Luke snickers from behind his two giant paper sacks of groceries as he passes his way through the living room to the kitchen. I stand back a few feet with the bag of sprays. I got them all: cleaning sprays, bug sprays, disinfectant sprays, bathroom sprays. As cozy as this place is, it's a tad rustic. I wasn't going to do this cleaning thing in vain. I want this place to feel like a home, but that is not why I hang back. I'm also not quiet because of the spider. The spider was not fun, but I work outside. I've seen a few of them in my life. It mostly just startled me.

Nate always teases me that he can tell when my heart is uneasy. I think it's because when I'm unsettled, I allow other things, like spiders, to affect me so much more than normal. Maybe it's a twin thing, but Nate would have picked up on my somberness and extra jumpiness by now.

I've never been good at guarding my heart.

Luke and I still haven't talked about what happened in Vegas. I know the saying, "What happens in Vegas, stays in Vegas." I caught some major feelings, and I brought them home. However, we fell right back into our same old lives, where I went to work, and he went to school. We acted like two awkward roommates with Boston tagging right along.

Except I'm not the same.

Now I have this new toxic trait that every time my mind stills, it instantly goes back to Luke kissing me in front of the Eiffel Tower. I can blame all the hand-holding, dancing, and even most of the flirting on the charade and trying to get good photos, but that kiss undid all my past assumptions of Luke. It was so much more than just erasing the bad, it was so potent, it branded my lips. Now I walk around feeling like not only do I belong to him, but I long for another kiss like that so badly, my heart aches.

Every time I think about it, I blush so hard my scalp even heats.

I want to talk about it.

I want to confess, every time I'm near him, my breath hitches so hard I must remind myself to take actual breaths.

Every time I try to open my mouth, my heart squeezes tight. I need this living situation to work out. At least until I can find someplace cheaper to rent. I don't want to risk making this more awkward. What if I tell him how I feel, and he cringes? What if he decides he can't live with me knowing I feel this way?

Luke is all the way in the kitchen. He sets the bags on the counter and as he pivots, he sees I'm still back by the front door, and his brow lowers. "What's wrong?"

I adjust my expression to avoid leaking out any truth and force my feet forward. "Just ah, you know—"

"Worried about the spiders," he cuts me off as his lips slide into an easy grin. One that's sweet but not condescending. "I told you. I can handle all the spiders. Give this place a good cleaning, and a day or two for them to get used to people being here, and they will all scurry away."

Pinching my lips together, I join him in the kitchen as he removes the ingredients for sourdough. I didn't believe it for a moment that he bakes bread, but he seems content to drag out his joke. I set my bag next to his, and take out my sprays one by one, stowing them under the modern kitchen sink. "You know, if you are trying to prove you can make sourdough, so I don't text any guys, you don't have to worry about that."

"What?" His dark brows furrow, and he freezes with his hand hovered over the sack.

"You said you don't want to be home making sourdough while I'm sending guys pics. If you are trying to prove some point, you don't have to."

"About that." He runs his hand through his hair, spiking it up in the front. "I didn't mean to sound possessive or controlling, but I meant what I said. If we are going to live together and tell my parents we are together, nothing good is going to come from us dating other people. People will see it. Rumors will start. I can't have you living in my house if you're sneaking out with Don. You're not on the market. You're pending in my cart."

"Again, Don is just my boss," I blurt out, a little anger bubbling in my chest. I don't want to date anyone, and I see where he's coming from, but what I want to say is, "I don't want to be pending in his cart." How could I possibly explain what is going on in my heart? I just can't risk things getting more complicated. I play it safe. "I think it's fair, if we are living together, we won't date anyone. Plus, I don't have time to date anyone. I plan on working a lot to save money."

"Okay, then." Luke's lips slide into a satisfactory position as he resumes to remove the groceries, grabbing the bag of flour. "I'm still going to make sourdough though. This has absolutely nothing to do with Don."

I bite back a chuckle, and the extreme level of Luke's stubbornness sinks in. I decide it's best not to bring up the kiss. Instead, I grab my cleaning spray and a roll of paper towels, and head toward the door, calling back, "I'm off to clean."

Right before I get to the door, my stubbornness kicks in, and I slip my phone out of my pocket, and set it on the counter in front of him, screen up. "You can hold on to this, so you know I'm not off texting someone while you're baking your bread."

"Are you sure you don't need it in case your work needs to get ahold of you?"

"I'm sure." I swallow, weighing all my options. I could just smile sweetly and walk away, but my heart is so unsettled having this chemistry between us, and nobody is saying anything, and I bleep out, "You're the only man I want to talk to anyway." Then I pull my shoulders back with sass and leave him with that.

After spending my night deep cleaning most of the downstairs living space, I head upstairs to the only bathroom in the house to get ready for bed. I find the bathroom shower recently used, with water droplets still on the door. I slip inside, accepting that as a cue to take a long shower, since Luke's already had his. It hasn't sunk in yet, that I'm actually going to be sleeping in this place. Yet I'm going through the motions, trying to get used to my new normal.

As I scrub up, I stress over all my anxieties. I'm used to sharing a house with a roommate. Nate and I lived together our whole lives, so I'm hoping that part isn't so different, but I can't deny this would be a lot less nerve-wracking if I didn't have so many unsettled emotions. Sighing, I shut off the water and step out of the shower. I guess it's one of those things that needs time to work itself out.

I get dressed and return downstairs, whistling a Christmas song that got stuck in my head. When I'm right outside my bedroom door, I halt on my heels. Luke is casually coming out of my room, wearing a pair of athletic shorts and a plain white T-shirt. His hair is damp on the edges. If I had to give a single word to describe how he looks when his gaze meets mine, it would only and ever be a *thirst trap.*

Okay, that's two words, but I'm stunted and can't do the math.

"Hey." His jawline seems to be growing stronger every day, like he's taking up some daily mewing habit, it practically glows under the muted evening light. His lips slide up into an easy grin. "I checked your room for spiders again, and you are all set."

I'm pretty sure my heart winks back.

"Bahahaha! I mean . . . thanks." I tilt my head, pretending to scratch an itch on my ear as my mind struggles not to think about all the things.

"I have an 8:00 a.m. final exam tomorrow, so I'm heading to bed. Unless you think you need anything else?" He lifts a brow, pinning me into place.

"Need anything?" I echo and shuffle my feet back involuntarily, doing everything to keep my lips from blurting out that a good-night kiss might be nice.

Yeah, I would never ask for that.

Oh, but that jawline.

"I'm good," I manage as his smile softens, reminding me of how easy it was to fold my lips into his.

Stop. It. Noelle.

I pull my shoulders back and force a business expression because that's what this is—a mere business transaction.

"All right then." He strolls forward toward the staircase, calling back, "Night, Noelle."

"Night, Luke." He disappears up the stairs, and I let out the breath I was holding.

I finally understand why they call it being a grown-up. I've developed this daily habit of groaning when I wake up. Pulling one eye open, my gaze pauses on my alarm clock. I'm already running late for work, and I haven't even gotten out of bed yet. I can't believe I slept so hard. I don't remember waking up even once. As my eyes come more into focus on my surroundings, I recall I'm now living in the chateau. I abruptly sit up straight, listening for the sounds of Luke outside my door.

Silence.

Folding my bottom lip in, I ease my feet down to the bare floor, and quietly pad to my door. My heart ticks up a notch as I press my ear against it and listen once more.

Silence.

He's probably already in town.

I let out a breath of relief, unsure of why I'm so tense at the mere thought of running into him. I'm clearly in an adjustment period and need some time to get used to everything.

It's just Luke.

Who cares if I run into him?

I twist my doorknob, pull my door open, and involuntarily hold my breath as I scan the room.

No Luke.

Swiping my hand across my forehead, I scold myself for acting so immature. It's not a big deal. Just get ready for work so you don't get fired. That's the bigger concern, I pep-talk myself.

As I cross the living room enroute to the bathroom, a warm scent, unlike anything I've ever smelled, wafts under my nose. It's a tad sour, maybe potato*ish,* but oddly appetizing. Without hesitation, I pivot toward the kitchen. I push past the swinging kitchen door and freeze.

A perfect mound of sourdough bread rests on the wood cutting board in the center of the stove with a note. My eyes narrow suspiciously, and I stride forward until I can read the boxy penmanship.

Just holding up my end of the deal.

My gaze slams to the heavens, and I let out my second groan for the day.

How did this even happen? There's no way it's done already. I've seen YouTube videos about this bread. You have to make a starter and feed it a bunch. There's no way it's done already.

Yet here it is. Looking amazing.

I can't eat it though.

My gaze traces the crust. All formed into the perfect little ball and marked with a cross on top, still wafting off a warm fresh oven vibe.

I mean, I could eat it.

I pinch my lips together and bite back a smile.

Never mind, I'm trying the bread. I march forward, yank a knife out of the block, and saw off a healthy slice. Before I stop myself, I take the largest bite, and like I'd suspected, it's sourdough perfection. Not that I even know what sourdough is supposed to taste like. This is the first time I ever recall trying it, but it's a slice of sourdough heaven.

I shove another bite through my teeth and shake my head as I murmur to myself, "If this is what marriage is, who wouldn't sign up for this?"

Eighteen

Luke

I made it through a full day of final exams without even remembering what I wrote the essay parts on, and then I drove to the stable to meet Noelle. Slowing as I pull into the gravel clearing outside the gate that surrounds the stables, my wheels noisily creep to a stop. It's enough noise to draw Noelle's gaze toward me, as she crosses the pasture with a small white horse beside her. Her face turns to me at the same time her brow pins together, and she waves, calling, "Hey, you! Are you riding today?"

"No." I shut my car door behind me and walk forward, putting a foot up on the bottom of the gate as it's locked from the inside, and I can't go any farther. "I'm hoping I can help you load up Buttercup, and we can take him home tonight."

"Tonight?" Her perfect pink lips part into a pause, showing me all those perfect bottom row teeth, before she breaks out into a beaming smile. "Are we ready for that?"

Tossing my shoulder up, I add, "Yeah, why not? The barn's been empty for years. It might have some mice, or maybe a spider or two, but I'm sure we can handle it."

Her perfect top teeth come down, biting her bottom lip as she appears to be suppressing a happy scream, but all the noise she doesn't make lights a firelight in her eyes. They beam back at me with so much sparkle, I can't help but marvel at how beautiful she is. "Let me put Buster back in his pen." She gives the white horse a soft pat on the side of his swollen belly. "Then I'll let Buttercup know the good news."

"Sounds good," I call over the fence, before tacking on, "I assume you have a horse trailer we can hook up to your truck. I doubt he will fit in my car."

"Yeah, I do, and he's great about riding in it, so it won't be too hard. You really don't need to stay to help. I load him up all the time, and he rides well."

I'm not a huge horse person. I think my grandpa's attitude about them might have rubbed off on me a little, but I want to stay. Everything about this moment feels like it's special. We are bringing Noelle's most prized possession—and friend—to *our home*. Of course, I want to see her face the moment Buttercup sees his new home. I wouldn't miss that for anything. "If it's okay with you, I would love to stay."

"Sure." She takes a sideways step, leading Buster closer to the pens. "I'll talk to Don first to see if I can buy enough feed from him to get me by until I can get to the feedstore."

"Sounds good." I nod, excitement bubbling in my gut. "I'll wait in my car."

"It shouldn't be too long." She's already speed walking Buster across the pasture, and I back away from the gate with a full grin on my face. If having Buttercup at the chateau doesn't make Noelle happy, then I don't know what will. I'm so glad I can help her out this way.

I climb back in my car, and rest my head against the headrest, my eyes instantly growing heavy. It's been a grueling week. Having that trip to Vegas where I got no sleep, and then moving into the house, and now rolling right into final's week. My body is feeling the strain of the nonstop movement. It will be good once Buttercup is moved, and then things will slow down, at least until next semester starts, but I have a few weeks.

My chest fills with air as I inhale the longest breath, and it feels so good to finally be all the way done with school for this semester. I can let go of all that stress, and just go home. My eyelids drift and beg for just a little rest.

Errrt!

I jolt backward as my eyes pop open.

Noelle's racing toward me, her truck parked behind me, pulled over with the driver's door wide open like she had fled. The trailer is hitched up, but the back horse gate is open.

So not a good sign.

Buttercup isn't in the trailer.

My eyes follow Noelle's path of trajectory right to Buttercup, who is charging toward me.

This is my chance to impress her!

He's coming right this way.

If I can get to him first, I can rescue him. I can already see Noelle's gorgeous dark lashes batting at me as she thanks me for being so brave.

Yanking on my door handle, I jump out of my car, ready to race after Buttercup. Everything is falling into place as I planned. Not only is my car door blocking his path, but he's also coming right this way. I stand next to my door, using it like a barricade, and I jut my foot out, ready to dart forward.

Here's the part I massively miscalculated.

He's racehorse *fast* and leaps over my open car door, but he doesn't clear it. Instead, he belly flops onto it, and he yelps as he bounces.

Noelle screams in the distance, calling for Buttercup, "Buttercup! Stop!"

Buttercup's not done.

He kicks his legs until he drops down on the other side of my car but not before his back hooves smash right through my driver's window, shattering the glass to the ground. I suck back a huge dizzy breath and resist the urge to drop to my knees to weep.

My car is my baby.

That stupid horse.

Gritting my teeth together, I snarl as I now have more than one reason to grab this rogue horse. *He's not getting away from me.* Rocketing forward, I smoke right past Noelle, not stopping until I'm next to Buttercup, and can slip my hand around his hanging reins. I wrap my fingers around the leather and gently tug it to slow him down.

He's not really into that.

Instead, he pulls more speed, and I must dig deep to keep pace with him as we charge forward together, I yank back on his reins, but he's not even fazed.

I trip.

Which, I should add, under the circumstances was quite a manly trip, but Buttercup's running free to greener pastures, and I can't get my footing. Now, he's dragging me alongside him, and I struggle to not let my feet slide under him, as I'm desperate to not get trampled on.

"Stop, Buttercup!" Noelle wails from way back by my car.

"Yeah, stop!" I holler through clenched teeth as I cling for dear life. "We aren't going to hurt you. You are going to a new house."

Let's say he's not my biggest fan, and he whips his head back, jerking the bridle with him, and once again, I cling to the reins.

I also pray I don't die!

I'm going to have to let go!

I can't survive getting run over by this beast.

That means Buttercup gets away.

And that will break Noelle's heart.

Only now, it looks like it's my fault Buttercup gets away, and I can't have that.

She'll never forgive me.

Oh no!

I can't have that at all.

I roll my clenched fists in and use all my upper body strength to pull myself up. I can't run as fast as Buttercup, and I don't care to even risk it again, but I can try something else.

I fling my leg up onto his belly, and wrap the other one around the other side, so I'm straddling his side. Now, using all my strength, I pull on the bridle to shimmy up.

It seems so much easier in my head.

It takes so much strength to hold on, as the horse races forward, and I struggle to hold my head up, trying to inch to the top of this thing.

I'm slipping, sweating, and close to tears.

My palms are soaked in perspiration, and the bridle is not that easy to climb. Every time the horse bounces off the ground, I jolt hard, and I cinch all my muscles tight to not fly off.

What I wouldn't do for a stuntman.

I'm going to die impressing this girl.

"Luke!" Noelle screams, her voice cracking in terror. "Just let go. You are going to get hurt."

I could.

But even letting go seems like it would be painful at this point.

I grind my molars, mustering up every ounce of strength I have, and groan as I heave myself up, and reach one arm over his back. This would be so much easier if he had a saddle on because it would give me something to grab, but I hug his body as tight as I can and hoist myself up onto his bare back.

It's still not a time for deep breaths and celebrations, because Buttercup is clearly not happy. I adjust my grip, and pull back on the reins, but he bucks his back as he slows. I tug again, digging my heels hard into his belly and holler, "Whoa, whoa!"

Maybe he finally wore out, because he responds to my second kick and stops.

I'm panting.

He's still a statue as we both wait for Noelle to catch up.

Tears stream down Noelle's face as she jogs over and takes the reins from me. As soon as she has them, I willingly slide off Buttercup, ready to give this beast back to her control.

I'm so over horses.

I don't care if I never see another one in my life. My brow is angled down, and I snarl my lip back at the beast while I huff out, "That was uncalled for."

"I-I, thank you so much." Noelle swipes her tears with one hand, as she brings her free arm up around Buttercup's neck and holds him close. Instead of scolding him for becoming possessed, she softly speaks to him, "Don't scare me like that."

Her gaze cuts to me, and I struggle to not run my mouth. I'm fuming mad, and I open and close my mouth, biting back all the words of hate I have for this horse.

Maybe I sent mixed signals by opening my mouth? I'd like to think it is my dashing heroic charm that lures her to me. Before I have time to close my mouth a second time, Noelle drops her hand from Buttercup's neck and takes a single step to close the gap between us, and plants a warm kiss in the center of my lips.

I step back, not because I don't want to kiss her—I want nothing more than to stay in a lip lock all day—but unfortunately, I'm still drained of my breath. I'm afraid I'll pass out. My heart motors up a notch, and I blink back at her.

"Sorry," she mutters as her gaze slams to the ground. "I don't know what came over me. I just felt so much gratitude."

"Don't be sorry," I rasp, longing ripe in my tone. "I just need a moment to breathe. It's exhausting being that brave." Our gazes lock together, and I suck in a long deep breath, knowing it's the most important breath I ever inhale. I wrap my arm all the way around her waist and tug her tightly to me as I lower my chin, teasing what's about to happen.

She doesn't pull away.

I take my time as I wrap my lips around hers and melt into her softness. Her breath is hot, but not as rushed as mine, and it brings all the tingles. From the depths of my being, I pour every bit of tenderness into this kiss. I want her to see stars when I'm done, but unfortunately, I'm still lightheaded. I'm the one who is about to see stars, and I pull away before I pass out.

Her fingertips fly up to her lips as she slowly smooths them, and she whispers, "I'm sorry about your car."

"Car?" I grunt out. "I can't even remember what my car looks like," I joke as I struggle to hold my rizz. "I'm sure it will be fine."

She laughs lightly, and we both stare at each other for another lingering moment before she says, "I think that's enough excitement for the day. I'm ready to head home."

Home.

There was never a more beautiful word spoken out of this woman's lips. Despite the pulsating soon-to-be-bruise on my legs begging me for mercy, I grin. "Let's go home."

Nineteen

Noelle

I balance two mugs of piping cocoa on a tray and try to smoothly glide my feet forward through the swinging kitchen door into the living room. Luke is sprawled out on his back on the sofa, one arm hanging down to the floor with the other hand securing an ice pack to his head. □

He's stripped down to shorts, and I try my best to keep my gaze from roaming over him. "How are you doing?" I ask, my attention remains on balancing my mugs.

"Other than pulling every muscle in my body, I think I'm on the mend."

"I'm so sorry," I rush out, heat flooding my cheeks as I'm overcome by guilt. "Buttercup has never done anything like this in his life. It's almost like he was showing off or something." I lower my tray to the coffee table and take one mug and hover it above him. "Maybe I should get you a straw?" I tilt my head, assessing how flat his body is against the couch.

"I can sit up." He winces as he pushes himself to a more upright position and takes the cup from me. "Thank you. I appreciate it."

"No problem. I don't know how you like it, but I used the packets that you bought from the store." I take the other mug for myself and sit across from him, on the fireplace hearth. I had tried to start a fire, but I'm not a Cub Scout. The only fireplaces I've ever started are ones with switches and gas. My fire is more smoking than it is flaming but I tried. Speaking of smoke, I cough as a wisp of it tickles my throat. I quickly mute it by taking a slow sip of my hot cocoa. Rich chocolate rolls over my tongue, and I swallow and let out a sigh after I swallow. "Mmm, that's good."

He cradles the cup between both hands, an expression of content stamping his face. "I know it sounds silly, but I firmly believe that hot chocolate tastes better in this cabin. I used to think my grandma had a special blend, or maybe she added secret spices, but she confessed she only ever bought the budget store brand. I've tried every brand there is, but I've never gotten it to taste like this. It's something about this place."

The velvety notes of chocolate hang on the back of my tongue, and I can't argue.

"So, you have yourself a horse that likes to drag people around." Luke's tone is teasing.

I cringe hard, doing my best not to hang my head. "I know he loves to pull things, but today was an eye opener and sort of a huge letdown."

"How do you mean?"

"It's not a secret that if I stay in Mapleton—which I need to do to keep Buttercup—I'm going to need a side hustle after we are done with this arrangement. I can't make enough at the stable. I've thought about it a lot, especially lately. I was thinking I could start a business with Buttercup, and then his boarding expenses would actually be a tax write-off. I could take him to fairs and pumpkin patches and things to have kids pay a few bucks to ride him. But after seeing how he was with you; I have to scratch that idea. I can't imagine how badly I could be sued. So, it's back to the drawing board. I guess I can get a waitress's job or something."

"I'm not a lawyer yet but this is as good as legal advice, don't let anyone ride him—ever." His head bobs up and down. "But he is a strong workhorse. Maybe you can find a different way to use his talents?"

"I don't know what. It's not like people use horses to pull wagons anymore." I take another sip of hot chocolate, forcing my brain to think about something that isn't so depressing. "Maybe I'm wrong, but I've always felt it deep in my gut that I was supposed to work with horses, but if that's truly the case, I wouldn't need two jobs and a free housing situationship to afford it."

"It will get better as you get more experience." He holds my gaze, his tone warm and encouraging, "Things take time. You are starting from scratch. It's not like someone is handing you a stable for free. I admire what you're doing."

I scrupulously tilt my head to the side, calling his bluff. "You do?"

"It's hard work, physically and mentally," his voice firm. "If you compare it to my life, I selected law school because it's easy. I mean the school isn't easy, but the path is. My dad has a firm, and I don't even have to look for a job. I'll start with a great salary, and the only real struggle I have is getting through school. I have a lot of privilege, which I understand and I'm grateful for, but I'll admit what you are doing is more exciting."

"Interesting. Did you always want to be a lawyer like your dad?"

"No, I would prefer to work with wood, hand-carving specialty projects. My grandfather trained me years ago, and that's part of why this place is so special. He used these very trees for wood, and I always thought I'd do the same. However, as I got older and realized how much stuff costs, it became clearer that woodworking would be more of a hobby."

"It has to be difficult to not follow your dreams. I can't stop thinking about mine."

"Well, again I think it comes down to lifestyle. When I think about my life, I want to be able to have all the things. Not from a materialistic standpoint, but I love this house, and it's in dire need of repairs and upgrades. That costs money. I'd love to have a big family. Lawyers make a good living, and if I want to someday afford a sassy brunette and a yard of fluffy cows, I need the money to do it."

"Fluffy cows?" I hike a brow as that seems out of nowhere.

"Yeah, I'm not a huge horse person but I do love animals." His lips spread into a full smile. "Who doesn't love a fluffy cow?"

"I didn't realize you thought that much about that stuff."

"Ah, I already have my cow's name picked out. It's going to be Seamus."

"That's an interesting name. Where did you hear that?"

"It means God hears, and plus it just sounds tough. I always envisioned having at least one, if not a small herd out here." Luke's eyes take a faraway expression as he looks past me. "As for the house, I know I must have seemed desperate to con you into this scam. It wasn't so much about the possibility of me not getting the house, but Rob wouldn't love it the way I do, and he's definitely not someone who just appreciates the countryside more. That's what this house needs."

"I'm glad I can help."

He strains his neck, leaning forward to sip off the edge of his cup. I cringe at how hard it looks. "I'm so sorry about today," I awkwardly blurt out. "Well, not sorry about all of it." I gesture with my hand. "Mostly I'm sorry about your car, and Buttercup. Not sorry about the kissing part—" I halt as soon as the last part is out, and clamp my bottom lip, wondering if I should apologize again for being awkward. ☐

"It was nice but just unexpected. I didn't think we'd be doing that, but yeah, I don't mind unexpected stuff, I guess."

He snickers with pinched lips as he struggles to hold in his hot cocoa, and when his Adam's apple bobs down in a swallow, his lips part, and he says, "Ah, that was smooth."

"Right." I laugh it off, but it's still the only thing on my mind. "I didn't mean to put you on the spot, but it's just a thing that happened. I don't want you to think I'm sorry about that. I'm not. I actually really enjoyed—"

"I'm not sorry about it either" he says, his gaze boring into me. "And you're right. I wasn't expecting it either, but it was nice."

"Well good." I add a nod, asserting our agreement that we are *not sorry* for the kissing. I still don't know what this means. I don't want to appear too needy, since he's already endured so much for me. "So." I tap my foot on the floor and look around the room. It's rather warm here now, despite the fire mostly surviving my feeble attempt to make it work. "I got Buttercup in the barn. He was rather agreeable to the move once he saw it. It's roomy."

"That's good." He takes another sip of his hot chocolate before his eyebrows raise. "Oh, before I forget. My mom invited us over for Christmas Eve dinner. I didn't accept. I wanted to see what you thought first."

"Christmas Eve," I echo, doing the math. "Boy, that's in two days, isn't it?"

"It came fast this year."

I've been so worried about having a roof over my head that I forgot about the holidays. "I don't think I have anything planned. I can go to my parents' on Christmas Day if your mom needs to see us on Christmas Eve."

"Yeah, I know we aren't married, but we at least need to keep up appearances for a while."

"Makes sense." I look down at my cup, as there is nothing special about this little white mug, but it oddly has been the most delicious hot cocoa I've ever had. Luke might think it's the house, but I suspect it's the company. When I raise my gaze, I find him lowering his eyelids, as if he's about to nod off. "Is there anything else you need to be comfortable before I head up to shower?"

"No, I don't think so, but thank you for taking care of me."

"It's the least I can do, considering it's all my fault, and well"—I pull my lips into a teasing grin— "isn't that what a wife is supposed to do?"

"I guess, I don't know because I've never had one before." His lips stay in a neutral position. "But just know I'm not taking it for granted."

"I know." I lower my lashes a tad shyly and stand. "I tried your sourdough."

"And what did you think of my culinary perfection?"

"It had good chew through." I nod as I downplay how absolutely amazing it was. "Great texture. I could get used to it."

"I'm glad it turned out." His easy grin did more to tell the whole truth than the words he left out.

"You bought it, didn't you?"

"How'd you know?"

"Do you actually expect me to believe that you bake?"

"I think I did."

I throw my head back and chuckle.

"I think I just got jealous." His perfect teeth come down on his lower lip, biting it. "Sorry."

"It's okay. This is a new thing for both of us, and neither one of us has an idea how we're supposed to act."

"That's true. They don't really write fake marriage rules."

"I mean, we could if we wanted to."

"Do you want to?"

"Nah, I trust you, and I sort of like seeing what happens." I swallow hard but hold my gaze.

"I trust you too." He looks down at his mug. "Well, I'm almost done, and I think I might try to sleep."

"You should rest." I stand up, taking a step toward the stairs, and calling back, "Holler if you need anything."

"Just one more thing."

I flick my gaze back to him, catching his smile as it tips into a rascally one. He lifts his mug toward me, and says, "Cheers to the unexpected."

Heat rushes to my cheeks as our eyes lock together, almost as if he is daring me. His expression draws tight, while he waits for my reply, but what am I supposed to say to that? It isn't the most platonic toast I've heard, as it's loaded with innuendo about us kissing more.

My heart thrums against my chest, as I lift my mug toward his, and simply say, "Cheers to the unexpected." I flash him my best flirty smile and walk away, maybe swaying my hips just a little.

Twenty

Luke

The next morning, I wake up not as soundly as I'm used to. In my immobility I had fallen asleep on the couch, and I jolt to a heart-pounding alertness when Noelle emerges from her room, stomping as if her pretty little feet are on *backward*.

How had I not noticed this less-than-perfect trait before?

I squeeze my eyes together, trying to go back to sleep, but her thumpity thumps go all the way up the stairs, and then back down again, at least four times. It is like she's part Frosty the Snowman.

"Morning," I grumble as she's on her second pass to the kitchen. Apparently, disorganization and running around like a crazy person is something she enjoys in the early mornings as well. "Can I help you find something?"

"Oh, sorry." Her lips pinch together as her gaze cuts to me. "Did I wake you?"

"No, not at all." My expression is still. "I just heard thundering and thought the house was exploding."

"It's not thundering out." Her lips curl with amusement in the corner. "However, it snowed a ton, and I'm not even sure I can get out of the driveway."

"The snowstorm must have come early." Craning my neck, I jerk my gaze out the front window. As far as my eyes can see lies a blanket of snow that somehow snuck in soundlessly during the night. Huge fluffy flakes fall fast but without force as they add to the majestic landscape. It has to be at least two feet, which isn't anything abnormal for this time of year, but it's crazy to be way out here in the mountains when it happens. "Ah, yeah." I process the snow. "I doubt we can get out. I'm going to need a tractor to move that much snow, and I don't have one."

"I listened to the morning news a bit, and they said plows are out, and snowmobiles are helping people get medications if they need it. They don't expect this snow to end for at least another day."

"So, we are snowed in."

"I guess. Good thing we got the little groceries we did yesterday. I'm really glad we brought Buttercup home last night, or I'd be worried sick about him stuck at the stables."

"How is he?"

"I haven't had a chance to check yet, but I need to."

"Oh, well hold up a second, and I'll walk you out."

"No problem." She motions to her T-shirt and points to her room. "I need to change into some warmer clothes first."

"No rush, as we can't go anywhere."

Her lips bend into a gentle smile, and she heads to her room. I take a moment to assess what's going on. We have a lot of snow. I'm feeling better, physically. Mentally, I'm a bit taxed with one thing on my mind.

Noelle.

I hate to do this, but I might need council on this one. I take my phone out to call Boston.

"'Sup, bruh," he answers on the first ring.

"Hear me out," I rush before he starts insulting me. "I'm snowed in with Noelle, and I'm so confused because she's flirting a lot."

"Interesting. Are you still in the friend zone?"

"Not the friend zone so much." I stand and pace to the kitchen, checking behind me to make sure Noelle isn't coming. "I think we've left the friend zone. We are kissing but not dating."

His hum reveals his thinking pattern. "So how much kissing?"

"I didn't measure it." My brows dip down, and I grouse. "More than once but not enough for me to think it's intentional. It's sort of been accidental kissing. But she doesn't pull away."

"I actually specialize in accidental kissing."

"You do?"

"I do. It means you are both in love with each other but too chicken to confess your feelings.

Love.

Phew. I blow out a quick breath and check over my shoulder again.

I blink, wishing I had started taking notes as that was quite a lot to digest. "Are you sure you know what you are talking about?"

"Bruh, I have five sisters, all older than me. I specialized in eavesdropping on all their phone calls. I'm not wrong."

I roll my lips in, weighing what he said. I've secretly held in my feelings and have been for years. That makes sense. If it means she's also doing the same thing, then that could be . . . I try so hard to hold in my smile as I hate to get my hopes up, but the mere thought of Noelle finally returning my years of unrequited love makes my whole face break out in a grin. "So, how do I get out of accidental kissing?"

"You could just tell her how you feel, or, with Christmas Eve being tomorrow, you could get a meaningful gift. Sparkly stuff always does a lot to mute a man's flaws for a woman."

"A gift is a great idea." I run a hand through my hair, and muse. "What should I get her?"

"So, gift wise, I'd get her something sentimental. Something she's shared about herself. A favorite perfume, perhaps. That tells her that you are tuned in, and it will set the stage for the next step. You take the reaction she has when she receives that gift, and you should be good to tell her how you feel. If you wait too long after the kissing starts, and you don't tell her how you feel, she will start to think you are using her. Don't be a wuss. Tell her now."

"Right." I nod, even though he can't see it. "I think I got it. Thanks."

I end the call. Goosebumps trickle up my spine, and I close my eyes, already dreaming how this could be the best Christmas ever. We are snowed in and forced to spend the day together, which is great. However, I can't leave to shop for a present with this snow. And ordering something online is out of the question. No UPS guy is going to be out on these hills today or any day soon. My heart drops. How am I going to get her the perfect gift?

"Are you ready?" Noelle calls from the living room, and I haven't even put on a coat or shoes.

"Yes, just getting my coat," I holler as I stow my phone in my pocket and open the fridge to grab a carrot for Buttercup, and then rush out of the kitchen. "Sorry, I was talking to Boston about the . . . *snow.*"

"We have enough of it, don't we?" The smile she gives me sends a spark right to my gut.

I hold up the carrot. "I'm bringing him a bribe to try to clear the air between the two of us. Hopefully, he doesn't hold a grudge."

"He very well could. He's an excellent judge of character."

I chuckle, loving how easy it is to tease her. "Need I remind you, it was you he ran away from first?" I wag the carrot at her like a disapproving finger, but she ducks and moves forward.

We pass through the door, the sting of winter instantly hitting my face. It hasn't been this cold all year, and it takes a moment to adjust. The snow is fluffy, not the kind that crunches when you walk. We sink knee-deep into it, and Noelle giggles as she struggles to plow forward. Her jaw drops as her rosy cheeks turn toward me. "Snow is in my shoe."

"I don't have any winter boots here either," I add.

Her mischievous grin grows on her face. "Maybe this is what we get because we toasted to the unexpected last night."

"Oh, so the snow is our fault," I eagerly flirt back as we trudge through the snow.

"Maybe we should have been more specific?"

"Now we know for next time. We don't want unexpected snow. Just unexpected kissing." I give her a wink right as we make it to the barn, and I unlatch the sliding door, cracking it open enough for us to slip inside.

"Ba ha!" Noelle bleeps out a noise I've never heard before. It's half crowish, but sort of cute. I love the way it makes her already rosy cheeks fire red. "That's a bold ask, don't you think?"

"I don't think so. I mean, you are my wife." I playfully shrug my shoulders, enjoying the way her eyes sparkle back at me. "I should be able to kiss you, right?"

Her gaze stills on me, but she doesn't reply. It's as if she's weighing the consequences of what her reply could mean. I admit it was a bit of a risky question, and it could go either way. My heart ramps up as I wait on her reply when a jingle sounds from behind me, startling us both. I whip around, scanning the open barn space. "What is that?"

Noelle's eyes are wide as they lock on me. "I was hoping you knew. Perhaps the wind blew something?"

We stare behind us. The wind is light, almost flirty as it flutters the snowflakes down in a playful pattern. I flick my gaze back to the house, making sure the door is shut tight, and it's not the squeak of the hinges. It's shut. With snow covering the entire landscape, there isn't so much as a bustling leaf on the ground.

Everything is silent.

Buttercup makes the first noise, snorting from his stall. It's so loud, it pulls us out of eye lock, and Noelle turns and strides toward him. "Hey, buddy. How was your first night in your new home?"

I stand back, breathing deeply as I study this exchange. Buttercup is calm, sticking his muzzle over the stall door and pressing it against the side of Noelle's face. "Too bad we can't play outside today." Her voice is smooth as she rubs the top of his muzzle. "But hopefully, the snow melts soon, and we can explore our new home."

"Hey, Buttercup." I risk a step forward, holding the carrot out as bait. "I brought you a treat." His humongous eyes stare as I ease forward another step, stopping a good arm's length away to reach the carrot under his mouth.

He whisks it out of my hand with a solid crunch. I pass a pleased smile to Noelle, and the jingle sounds again. This time it appears to come from above us. "What is that?" I assert, scanning the beams above us for an old forgotten toy or something.

"It almost sounds like music playing."

"Right, but from where?" My gaze finds its way back to Buttercup, but he's quiet, staring at me as if he's waiting for me to pull another carrot out of my pocket. Speaking of pockets, I push my hand inside and remove my phone, checking to make sure it's on silent. "Maybe an app or something opened on my phone?" My brows fall into a furrow as everything appears to be locked, and I sigh as I return it back to my pocket. "I'd say I'm hearing things, but you heard it too."

"I did." Her eyes grow fearfully large as she takes a step closer to me, dropping her tone. "You don't suppose it's like a sign from your grandma, do you?"

"Nah." I shake that thought off immediately. "Maybe we should head back to the house. We might be able to find out what it is on the way back."

"Ah, sure." Her gaze floats back to Buttercup as she leans in and gives him another hug. As she shuffles her feet closer to the door, she calls back to her horse, "I'll be back later."

We instantly synchronize our steps as we pass through the door, and I'm about to lock the door behind me, when we both spot something way out of place.

A little white and brown fluffy cow.

It's as if he was dropped into the snowbank, and his head barely peeps out. "Where'd he come from?"

"Oh, how adorable!" Noelle squeals as she rushes forward and leans over to pet him. "Did you get him just for us?"

He's tame, not fighting back at all, and he doesn't look cold, despite being almost buried in the snow. "Ah, I don't think I got him." I pass a look in the direction of the closest neighbor's house, a good quarter mile down the road. It's a rural area, and a cow isn't the strangest thing I've seen out here. "My guess is he got lost from next door."

Noelle's pursing her lips out, trying to give the cow little kisses. The cow is so tame and eats it all up. "Yeah, but wouldn't you see tracks from over that way?"

"You're right." I study the snow, not finding a single set of tracks except for the ones right where he's standing. "Maybe the wind covered them up right away?" I think aloud, as this snow is extremely fluffy and light. "There's nowhere else he could have come from. There haven't been cattle of any kind on this land in decades."

It's not like Santa just dropped him out of the sky.

A chill runs along my spine, and I covertly toss a look heavenward. Nothing but snowflakes falling so fast one finds my eyelash. I blink it away and shake off that thought.

Her lips form a giant O. "Look, he has a jingle bell on his collar. That's what we heard!"

"How funny is that?" The twist in my stomach calms as we solve the mystery. It all makes sense now, and I take a few light steps toward him, reaching out. "Hey, little guy. Do you want to come hang out in the barn until the snow melts? We can look for your family later, but it's too cold to hang out here." He's still, and I step forward again. He allows me to grab his collar, and I guide him back through the barn doors. He's so easygoing, acting as if he understands me. Maybe it's his way to avoid being meat, but he trots along right on my heels as I lead him into the stall next to Buttercup. "I hope they can get along with each other." I shut the gate to his stall and glance back at Noelle as she's still standing by the barn door.

"Buttercup's used to company, so he'll be fine. Besides, this cow looks like a conscious cow."

What did she say? I cock my head. "There is no such thing as a conscious cow," I tease as I return to Noelle, shutting the barn door again.

"I'm not so sure. He seems mighty aware of what's going on."

"Yeah, he does." I lower the latch on the lock, contemplating how weird this day is. "Well," I'm hesitant to reveal what I have to say, but I push through it. "A cow was unexpected."

"So unexpected but *good*." Noelle's eyes are wide as we trudge back through the snow.

I wag my brows at her. "Yeah, it's goodish. But not as good as other unexpected things."

Noelle throws her head back and laughs a hearty laugh, and her eyes sparkle back at me when she replies with a flirty smile, "With the way this day is going, nothing will surprise me."

I match her flirty smile and consider that an invitation.

Twenty-One
Noelle

It's looking as if we will be snowed in for Christmas. There's not much to do, so I take it as the perfect opportunity to take a long bath, with the stereo blaring my favorite Christmas tunes. Yes, I brought a piece of sourdough lathered in butter and a mug of hot chocolate to the tub with me.

You only live once.

I chew the last bite of my bread and lower myself into the bubble bath until only my nose and eyes poke out. It's been a long time since I was able to fully relax. Even when I was living with Nate, I still had the constant pressure to make rent, and I never noticed the stress having Buttercup so far away was putting on me. It's amazing knowing he's just across the yard, and I can check on him whenever I want.

When I'm done with my bath, I slip on my Walmart muumuu nightgown and pad downstairs. I'm carrying my hot chocolate, which is now tepid at best, but oddly it still tastes amazing. I have a whole day ahead of me with no work, and nothing to do. Pursing my lips out, I muse about what I'm going to do with my time, and the niggling in the back of my head keeps reminding me tomorrow is Christmas Eve, and I'm snowed in with Luke. Our Christmas will be here—together.

The mere thought of it feels extremely magical, especially after our trip to Vegas, but I'd love to set the ambiance of the house a little more. When I was cleaning up yesterday, I found a large closet in the hallway that had random seasonal items in it. Everything from extra beach towels to mouse traps, and if I'm not mistaken, I remember a box labeled, "Christmas."

I pivot, and stride down toward the closet, an idea forming in the back of my head. I whip open the closet door again and locate the small box, just where I had remembered it. I shimmy it out of the bottom, doing my best to not have anything topple out of the closet. Once clear, I open the top. Just as I had thought. Garland and a few nicknacks. It's not nearly enough to decorate the whole house, but it is the perfect amount of stuff to decorate the mantel above the fireplace.

I pick up the box and stroll back to the living room, right as my phone rings on the coffee table. The caller I.D. shows Nate. "Merry

Christmas Eve Eve," I answer, relieved to finally talk to him again after so many days of hearing nothing.

"Merry Christmas Eve Eve to you too." A chuckle infuses his tone. "How are you?"

"Good." I nod, scanning the living room, not finding Luke anywhere. I didn't pass him on the way downstairs, so the only other place he could be is outside. I cross the room to the window, squinting into the bright white abyss. "I'm sure you heard Mapleton got snow. Luke and I are snowed in, and I won't be coming home for Christmas."

"I did not hear that, but I did hear something else that's super fascinating."

"Oh really?" I strain my neck, eyes focused on the barn. The door is cracked open, and if I had to guess, Luke's outside checking on the animals again. "What is that?"

"Did you elope?"

Clamping down on my bottom lip, I'm on the struggle bus to not blurt something out. I hadn't thought this far. I knew we were going to lie to Luke's family, but are we lying to my family? Nate and Luke talk all the time. It only makes sense he would find out.

What do I do?

Do I let him in on the secret or not?

I take a second to slowly swallow, before I open my mouth wide to inhale an extra dose of oxygen, and muster up my best innocent voice, "*Sure.*"

"Sure? What kind of reply is that? So, it's true?" His voice grows deeper. "I thought you couldn't stand Luke. Did I miss something?"

Ah, the thoughts that must be running through his head right now force me to hold back a giggle. I'm not in a position to let him in on this secret now, or it will ruin everything, and it's been going so smoothly. "Maybe." I pinch my lips together, trying so hard not to leak another detail out. I hate lying, but I also will get in serious trouble for letting the truth out.

"Can I ask how that happened?"

"We went to Vegas last weekend, stopped in at one of those quickie wedding chapels." I exhale, knowing both of those statements are facts. No lie there.

"Did you hit your head before that happened?"

"Nope. I was feeling quite well." My voice pitches higher, and I close my eyes, so afraid of where this is going. I need to end this call now.

"Look," Nate rushes out, his voice not seeded with compassion. "I have to tell you something. I have known Luke's been in love with you for years, but I never told you because you always made it clear you couldn't stand him. If you did this out of spite or something to get back at me, that's cruel because Luke genuinely loves you."

The word love pings right to my heart, and I freeze with one hand on the windowpane. "So . . . you love him?" Nate's word pace is abnormally slow. "Or are you using him?"

"I l-l." It's so soon to say the word love, and I can't get it out. I haven't even said it to Luke. How can I say something so sensitive to Nate? I rush to cover my blunder as sweat slaps on my back. "I mean, we got married. So that tells you how I feel."

"What is going on, Noelle?" Nate interrupts. "You're up to something because nothing about this seems real. You can't go from hating someone so much to getting married in a week. You are using Luke for his money."

"No—"

"Because if you are, and I find out, I'm telling Luke everything. About how you can't stand him, and how you are only there because I forced you to—"

"That's not it at all!" I blurt out, my cheeks filling with rage heat. "Don't you dare say anything about that to him."

"Noelle." His tone is extra curt.

"What?"

"I'm going to find out what's behind this."

Squeezing my lips together, I twist my face into my mad face and suppress a scream. I can't risk telling him, but if I don't, he might say something more damaging to Luke. My hand is shaking when I mutter back into the phone, "I'm not going to fight with you this close to Christmas, Nate. Have a nice holiday." I end the call, knowing there is only one way to solve this.

I need to tell Luke everything, including how I feel about him now.

If what Nate said is true about Luke always loving me, then everything should be fine.

Actually, better than fine.

If Nate's being a jerk to get me to confess to what's going on, and he's lying about Luke loving me, then this could make our living situation so awkward. I really don't have a choice though. I also can't just blurt it out, as we've made so much progress, and I hate to ruin how far we've come. I'll tell him tonight after dinner, when we have a chance to relax for a while.

My stomach twists into a giant knot.

Twenty-Two

Luke

Wearing one of my grandpa's old flannel shirts and jeans, I've never felt more in my element than when I'm in my grandfather's old shop, standing in front of a piece of wood. Thankfully, Grandfather had a whole load of it still stored in the back of his workshop.

I looked it up online, and Santa's real sleigh was made from pine, but today I'm settling for some birch, because it is already harvested.

Ever since I got it in my head that I need to get Noelle the perfect Christmas gift and tell her how I feel, I've been more than a little unsettled. I can't even get to a Winn Dixie, let alone a mall with this storm. All I want to do is show her she's more than just another girl to me. I want our Christmas to be the most magical ever. I had the most random thought last night when she was talking about her dream of working with horses. Buttercup is not a horse that can be trusted for riding, but he's an excellent puller. She could have a small sled to pull kids around. That would be so much safer as the weight of the sleigh would slow him down, and kids would be strapped in.

The thought of being pulled around by Buttercup makes my low back throb, and I reach back and rub it, adding to my thoughts, preferably they can be strapped with helmets and football pads.

Anyway, as soon as I had that thought I knew what her gift would be. I'm making a sled for Buttercup. I don't have the time to make anything fancy, but it's the thought that counts, right?

I pull out my tape measure, stretching it out over the length of the wood to do the mental math of how big of a sled I can make with what I have. I'd like it to be big enough for at least two small kids, if not three. The first board comes in at almost four feet, and I smile as I move onto the next one.

I'm reminded of the time I broke my first tape measure. I was stretching it as far as it would go and pulled too hard. The tape came out of the holder, and I was devastated. I asked my grandfather if it went to heaven. I thought he would laugh at me, but he must have seen my sadness, because he reassured me it would be there. I can laugh about it now, but more of those memories come flooding back as I move to the next board, and I know in my heart that doing what I did to save this chateau was right.

It's not just the house.

It's his legacy.

I can work in his shop—as he did—and bring wood art to life.

Not like his of course.

He had an other-worldly talent.

Or should I say, other-woody talent.

My lips slide into a full smile as sometimes my jokes are so corny I can't help but chuckle. Board number two comes in at just under three feet, and I keep moving down the line. I have eight boards. If I eyeball this correctly, I should be able to use six boards for the base, and two for the runners. It's going to be small. A lot smaller than I had hoped, but again, it's the thought that counts.

My phone vibrates right as I move to the fourth board, and I briefly glance at the caller I.D., seeing it's Dad.

"Hey, Dad," I answer, as I tuck the phone between my shoulder and ear and move to the next board. "How's it going?"

"I'm good, but I see the interstate is still closed. How are you guys holding up?"

"We are great. I finished my exams early on Tuesday, and we got enough of our stuff moved into the house. We even got Noelle's horse moved in before the storm came, which I'm glad about because I think she'd be worried about him. So, it's actually fairly peaceful." I stand up straight, casing the little workshop, feeling as if I'm exactly where I should be before I can't help but add, "I just love it here."

"It's good to hear you guys are well. It might be a few days before the snow stops, and they can plow everything out."

"Right. We'll have to schedule Christmas for when we get dug out."

"Oh yeah, that's no problem. The main thing is that you guys are safe. Oh, I had some interesting news."

"What's that?"

"Your cousin Rob's engagement is called off. I'm not sure what happened, but I guess you getting the chateau is meant to be, because he's no longer getting married."

My lips part, and I'm reminded of the dishonesty Dad still isn't aware of. Noelle and I have been getting along so well, I'd forgotten we are still lying to my parents. And now with Rob's engagement called off, technically there is no rush anymore to *be married.* "That's too bad," I muster up.

"Yeah, but it won't affect anything on your end. The house is already yours, and as I said, it seems like it is meant to be."

"Right." I swallow back a small lump in my throat. My conviction has been this house is meant to be mine, but today it's especially hard to keep my lie a secret. So much has changed since I first learned about Rob's engagement. Noelle was hardly even speaking to me. Now we are accidentally kissing, and it feels so amazing. Everything I ever wanted is falling into place. "We certainly are enjoying being here. I wouldn't have ever dreamed I'd be married before I graduated law school, but I can't imagine my life without Noelle."

That is the truth.

The hard truth I feel in my gut every time I think about when we go our separate ways. I just pray she falls for me before it's too late.

"Well," Dad sighs sleepily, "I'm going to take my nap. Do you want to keep us posted?"

"Sure." My gaze falls to the side. This is the first Christmas I'll be spending without my parents. It stings a little, and I rush to add, "Merry early Christmas. We will be in to celebrate as soon as we can."

"Sounds good, Son. Take care."

I end the call, and stare at my boards. I have enough to make a small sled, just the right size for a single horse to pull. It seems like that was meant to be too. My lips curl into a pleased grin. I can't wait to show Noelle what I made her.

My heart pinches tight against my chest wall.

I can't wait to tell her how I feel about her.

This is going to be the best Christmas ever.

I have no idea where the time went, but the sun is nearly setting when I add the final screw to the sled. I wish I had some varnish to finish it, but that's going to have to wait. My heart is beating so fast as I covertly pull the sled out of the little workshop behind the barn and sneak it into the barn, placing it in front of Buttercup's stall. He's unbothered by my presence, not even moving a step in my direction or away from me. "What do you think?" I point to the sled, speaking to him like we are old friends, and it feels oddly normal. "I got you and Noelle a present."

Of course he doesn't move.

However, the cow is pushing his head on his gate, trying to get a closer look. His little bells jingle. "At least you have the Christmas spirit." I grin as I walk closer to him. I've never seen a tamer cow. I stand in front of him, and he does nothing to put distance between us. He clearly must be someone's lost pet, and I reach my hand inside his stall. He actually brings his nose right up to my arm, pressing it down for petting. It's like this cow is a paid actor. He couldn't be any cuter. "Don't worry. As soon as the snow melts, I will find where you came from. Until then, you are welcome to stay here, where it's warm and you have food." I take a moment to rub behind his ears, and he pushes closer to me as if we've always known each other.

After another moment, I straighten up and take a step back, calling out to each of them, "All right, boys, you behave. I'll be back in the morning to check on you."

My grin is widespread across my face. I'm at ease simply closing the barn door, as if it's the most normal thing in the world, to head across the yard . . . *to Noelle.*

Fluffy flakes still flutter down and, oddly, it's almost like they *smell* like Christmas. It has an ambiance to it, especially when set with the chateau in the background and the woods behind that. I've spent a lot of Christmases in this house before, and each one always was the most exciting one. Never in life would I have dreamt

I'd have one like this. Just one year after my grandmother passed, and I didn't think I'd ever have a merry Christmas again. Here I am opening the front door, more excited than ever.

My eyes immediately land on the mantel, decorated with evergreen garland and white lights. A giant red ribbon is tied in the center of the garland and a small white Christmas tree rests on top of the mantel. I've seen that tree before. It's one my grandmother used to put on the hall windowsill, but it's the perfect fit where it is. "What is this?" I kick off my shoes and head toward Noelle.

"I hope you don't mind." Tiny pink flares spread under her freckles. "I got bored and thought it would be a fun surprise, since we have to spend Christmas here. Is it okay?"

"I love it." My gaze bounces from the mantel to Noelle. "It adds a nice festive touch." My eyes find the grandfather clock on the back wall, and I'm startled to see I was outside for eight hours. "Boy, I had no idea it was this late. Do you want something to eat?"

"I just ate a grilled cheese sandwich I made with your sourdough bread. It was amazing. Do you want one? I can make you one. The pan is still hot."

"That sounds good." My stomach churns as I already envision it as I move toward the kitchen. "I can make it."

"No, it's just grilled cheese. I know where everything is, because I just put it away. Why don't you go wash up, and I'll have it done in no time."

"If you insist."

"I do." Noelle's already disappearing into the kitchen, and I take my cue to head upstairs to wash.

Twenty-Three

Noelle

I don't cook.

However, everything about this house: the snow outside, seeing Luke walk in from working outside all day, and he's wearing his flannel shirt and work pants—it makes me want to know my way around the kitchen. I take the tea kettle, boiling with water, and fill two mugs. I'm already plating Luke's sandwich when he returns.

"One grilled cheese and an extra special hot chocolate." I offer him his plate, and he takes it. His gaze hovers over the long heirloom dining table across the kitchen before he takes a single step back and says, "That huge table feels so formal for just the two of us. Do you want to sit with me in front of the fireplace?"

"Sure." Nervous bubbles sputter in my gut, and I grab my hot chocolate and walk with him to the living room, where we both plop down in front of the large stone fireplace.

"My dad called when I was outside," Luke says right before he takes a hearty bite of his sandwich, drawing my attention to his lips, and I fight the urge to lean over to kiss him.

"What did he say?"

Luke slowly chews his sandwich in a thoughtful pattern, swallows, and says, "Rob's engagement fell through, so if he was going to contest me getting the house, he doesn't have any way to move forward now."

"Well, unless he gets a fake marriage, right?" I quip back, jutting him with my elbow.

"Yeah, but who does that?" His cackle is instant and contagious, and I join in. Flashbacks of us roaming Vegas in wedding attire trap my mind. The problem is there's no way I can think of Vegas without our moment—dancing in front of the Eiffel Tower—and that kiss. Goosebumps run along my arm.

I'm not supposed to goosebump for Luke.

This was never supposed to be like this. I'm sitting a few feet from him, and it's taking all my self-control not to lean closer.

I'm scared.

Really scared about how he's going to react when I confess to all the hurtful things I have said about him. Hopefully he understands I was being immature.

My stomach flips so hard, it's like I stumbled, but I'm not even moving when I open my mouth, knowing it's time. "I talked to someone today too. Nate called me. He heard about our marriage."

His eyes grow wide and dial in on me. "How'd he find out?"

"I didn't think to ask because I was so taken aback. Maybe your parents?" I tilt my head to the other side as I weigh the gravity of my forthcoming words. "Which means if my parents don't already know, they will be finding out shortly."

"You didn't tell them?"

"I-I was waiting to make sure everything works out before I brought them into this." I gesture toward him. "They love you. Always have. I'm not worried about that as much as the whole breakup part. Like, I think they'd get mad at me for that."

"The breakup part," he echoes as his eyes dance around my face. I can't pinpoint with accuracy what he's thinking, but his face drains of the warm glow it had into a bit of a pasty hue.

I run the pad of my thumb over my fingernail in a nervous fidget as I study him. "Are you feeling okay?"

His sigh is a blend of sweetness and frustration when his eyes hook mine. Slowly one corner of his mouth tips up into a lopsided grin. "Truthfully, I'm feeling better than okay—"

"Good," I cut him off, not because I don't want to hear what he has to say, but the spirals in his eyes speak so much faster than his words. I have to get my confession out before he says anything else. "I was talking to Nate about something else, actually. He reminded me of something."

"What was that?" His gaze dips to focus on finishing the last of his grilled cheese.

"You know you were always Nate's friend, and you spent a lot of time at my house?"

"Yeah."

"I hate to think about it now, especially since you've been so nice to me, but I said a lot of mean things about you." I swallow, and then rush the rest of the words out, "I'd take it all back if I could, but Nate doesn't believe we are married. He thinks I'm using you for your money. He threatened to tell you about how I used to complain about you, but I figured you sort of knew that already. I just don't want him to blow this for you." I pause and look down, adding, "I want you to hear it from me that I was actually really mean to you behind your back, but I was so stupid."

"You are using me. It is the plan. Right?" His serious gaze studies me. "We both are getting something out of the deal."

"Is it *still the plan*?" My heart twists like a rag and finds a way to crawl into my esophagus, where apparently, it's taking up residence as it thumps away.

"Are you asking what I think you are asking?" His eyes brim with loud curiosity as a stillness sets in, and the silence expands.

"It depends." I'm proud I can muster up a tiny bit of sass with my heart malfunctioning. I've never had a problem with my cardiac function before. Apparently, something is up. I grip the front of my throat and swallow, all the while my heart is literally beating out of my neck. "I, ah." My voice drops off, as I struggle with all the words that refuse to come out. I don't know what I want to say. Mainly I'm holding on to the fear Nate is going to do something to mess this—whatever it is—up with Luke before I have a chance to even figure out what it is, or what it could be. "I feel guilty about a lot of the things I said. I hope you know I'm not that person anymore."

"I know what you thought of me, but while we are on the subject." He dips his eyebrows, leaning in close. I suck in a long breath, trapping all my air in my throat as if my life depends on it while I wait. His face is so geographically close to mine, his warmth wraps around me, entombing me. I could stay here like this forever.

A highlight reel rolls in my head, replaying the moments we've shared, starting with our first kiss. The flashbacks stream back through these last couple of weeks, and I can't help but feel like I'm in a state of emergency. Like I'm speeding down a busy interstate trying to escape a wildfire, and I almost missed my exit, the most important turn to put me on my path to safety.

"Look, I'm not the best with words." His voice is raspy, framed by his jawline perfection. "Maybe that's why I never said anything all these years, but you had to know how I feel about you . . ."

Nate's voice telling me Luke loves me rings in my head. The thing is, I was so wrapped up in my own self, I didn't see anything to tip me off in the slightest. That really gives me a huge clue to how selfish I had been. I'm a moron. Had I known this is who Luke is, and how he'd treat me years ago, I wouldn't have resisted.

Now, I'm afraid I might have waited too long. "Luke." His name comes out with a pleading sigh. We are so close, literally butting up to a dam that's ready to break and flood out all the emotions we've both clearly been holding back. I widen my eyes, and yield, yearning for him to say what we both know we're feeling.

"My chest hurts whenever I look at you." He raises his palm to my cheek. A magnetic spark zaps the side of my face, instantly pulling me to him. Our lips crash together into an uncommonly slow kiss, the tingles spiraling around me like a vine sprouting new growth. When we pull away, our gazes entwine, lapsing into a comfortable silence. His thick lashes lower, fanning over his cheeks, as he presses his chin down to my shoulder and whispers, "I've always loved you." He says it like an oath but drops a heated sigh, adding in an assertive tone, "That's it. That's all I've ever felt, and I said it." He grabs my hand, pulling it close to him. "I don't care if it's not what you want to hear, but I'm tired of keeping it inside of me. I got bold with it."

My heart slams to a halt.

While my mind does it's best to rewind the hands of time all at once. If there was even a fog of a negative memory left in my brain, it was completely wiped away. Leaving me with a deep burning to do nothing but hold him. I've been told before that my hugs can be pretty magical, but nothing could have prepared me for the sonic boom that implodes in my chest. If this isn't love, then I don't know what else is and I tip my head back and whisper, "I love you too."

A loud scuffle from outside the front window sounds, alerting us both to our perfect surroundings, and as our gazes pull in that direction. All I hear is a soft jingle bell ringing. "Did the cow get out of the barn?" Luke rises to his feet, calmly pacing toward the window. I shuffle behind him, a little timid. I've never heard a noise like this before.

Pulling back the curtain, he peers out. The snow has finally stopped fluttering, but the sun is fully set over the horizon. The only light in the yard is the moon shining down and the small porch light. I come up behind him, peeking over his shoulder to scan the yard. No cow outside, and the barn door is closed. "I don't see either of the animals, but maybe I should check, just in case? They might have gotten out." Luke's gaze slides to me. Gone are the swoony inflections of his irises, and now nothing but serious flecks reflect.

"I'm going with you." I'm already pushing my way to the door.

"It's dark out, and you never know what it is. It might be a coyote or something dangerous."

"The something dangerous is the exact reason I'm going with you." I stuff my feet into my shoes as quickly as I can so he can't get ahead of me. "You aren't leaving me here by myself."

"Very well then." His eyes sparkle back at me for a mere moment before he drops a lazy kiss on the top of my nose and grabs his jacket, as he pulls open the front door. "Ladies first." His teasing grin tells me he's testing me.

I leak out a snort. "Ba ha ha. Not." I tuck behind him, holding my hands on his waist. "You aren't leaving me behind, but I'm fine following you."

He opens the flashlight on his phone and paces forward, allowing me to stay right on his heels. I shut the door behind us, and we cross the old creaky porch. The breeze is light and coated with pine pitch from the adjacent pine woods. "I don't see anything," I whisper as we descend the steps. Earlier the snow was fluffier and soundless, but as the temperatures dropped, the snow froze hard. Now it crunches beneath our feet, announcing our arrival.

"Everything looks normal." Luke's calm as we approach the barn, and he unlatches the door, pressing on the handle to slide it open. As he looks back at me, he reaches back, offering his hand. I don't waste a moment slipping my fingers into his. I take a moment to marvel at how wide his palms are as my fingers stretch all the way out and barely fill his palm. He's like a mountain man with his flannel shirt and his gorgeous strong hands, and they reassure me that whatever is in this barn, Luke knows what he's doing.

His jaw drops into an open-mouth stare. My gaze follows. At first, it's hard to see. The barn is dim inside, with the exception of mellow nightlight. To aid my adjustment, Luke switches on another light, and he waves me forward. "I spent the day making you a sled for Buttercup. He already proved he can pull, and I thought it would be a fun Christmas surprise that you might be able to turn into a weekend side hustle, but this is not what I made." His voice drops off as we approach a full-sized glimmering—yet antiquated— wood sleigh.

Balanced on two long runners, the wood appears freshly painted in a Christmas-cheery red. There is not a scratch in the finish, and it's donned in glowy hues under the barn light. It's about the size of a small car, with four seats split into two rows. Like a kid on Christmas morning, my jaw nearly hits the floor, the reverie lingering before my eyes. "You made this?" My voice steeps in awe as I move forward and run a hand over the smooth finish.

Shaking his head, Luke joins me next to the sleigh, appearing somewhat perplexed. He tosses a look over his shoulder, and then cranes his neck to glance up before finally drawing his gaze back to me. "I did not make this."

"I'm confused."

"Me too. I made you *a* sled. A much smaller sled that is closer to the ground. *This* I have never seen before, and I have no idea where it came from."

"It's Santa's sleigh." I tilt my head, peeking inside. Every inch of the surface is perfect, and I find myself climbing inside to take a seat. "It's amazing." I look back at Luke, and he's lingering, still looking confused. Clearly this is some silly act he's pulling on me, as he's pretending he's never seen this before. I'm not naïve. "I don't know what to say but thank you. I love it. I wasn't expecting anything like it, but it's amazing. You are amazing—"

"I didn't make it," he cuts me off, his voice pitching up. "I'm not lying about that. I made you a sled but *not this one*."

I pinch back a taut smile, as I know the game he's playing. He's so modest, and I'm not going to fight about it, and I decide to play along. "So, Santa just left it here then. Huh? That's crazy." I pat the spot next to me. "There's plenty of room. Come sit next to me."

He takes a clumsy step up onto the sleigh and drops down next to me while still jerking his head in all directions as if he's lost.

"Are you okay?"

"I'm f-fine." His gaze drops to me, and a curious smile buds. "Wait, you said you wanted a side business. Did you order a sleigh?"

I throw my head back, chuckling. He is good at acting. "You are something else."

His smile finally settles into his usual easy grin as his brow relaxes and he focuses on me. "I was really fooled there for a moment."

Shaking my head, I resist the urge to roll my eyes. He is adorable, putting this whole act on as part of my gift. It's seriously the most special thing anyone has ever done for me. "I have an idea." I give him the side-eye as I sway closer.

"I don't think it's safe to take it out for a ride now," he rambles as his eyes go wide in defense, and I let him go on for a moment longer as I bite my bottom lip, stirring up the courage. "Let's wait until the morning when we can see—"

I can't wait another moment. Sitting in this sleigh he made me for the best Christmas surprise is the swooniest thing I've ever experienced. It's Christmas magic and romance all rolled together. I'm overcome with joy and grab his shirt collar to pull him closer as I plant a kiss in the center of his lips. It only takes a moment for his lips to soften, and it quickly turns into one of those oxytocin hormone-producing kisses. His hand finds my cheek, and he kisses me back, filling me full of butterflies.

When I break our kiss, I breathlessly whisper, "Merry Christmas, Luke."

"Merry Christmas, Noelle."

"This is the best Christmas ever." I look down, finding his hand, and I pull it into my lap and tenderly squeeze it. "Thank you for everything, but especially the sleigh. I love it."

"I didn't make the sleigh," he huffs out, yielding his gaze over the dash.

"If you didn't make it, then who did?"

Our gazes slide together before rising above us.

And somewhere in the distance we hear a light jingle of bells.

Only our sweet fluffy cow is sleeping soundly in the corner.

Twenty-Four

One Month Later . . .

"Thermos of hot chocolate?" Luke calls out our inventory as we settle next to each other in our sleigh. Well, not next to each other. We have a small something between us. It's the perfect fluffy cow size to be exact. Our cow found his way between us, always our third wheel. After the great snow melted, he never went home. We asked all the neighbors around, but we never heard where he came from. It didn't take him long to own his space, and he never waits to be invited to hang out with us. We just know when we go for sleigh rides, he'll be there.

"Got it." I hold up the canister and tuck it next to me against the side of the sleigh.

"I have the blanket." Luke unfolds the heavy flannel over all three of us.

"We should be good." I pull back on the reins, and Buttercup takes off at a nice trotting pace over the pasture, away from our home. "How was your class this morning?" I ask, as I focus on steering Buttercup away from the ditches.

"Aside from the fact I'm sad to be back in school again, it was fine. I'm glad it's my last semester. I'll definitely be ready to graduate this May."

"Oh, aren't we supposed to break up in May?" My lips pull into an amused smile.

"It's too late for that." Luke pulls one arm behind my shoulder and dips his chin into my neck. "You had your chance to run. Now that I'm used to you, I'm never letting you go."

"That's a bold statement."

"It's true."

I give him a side-eye, warning of a sensitive topic. "So, if we aren't breaking up in May, are we going to let our family in on our little secret?"

His brows furrow together without adding sadness to his face. "I don't think we need to."

My heart sinks.

As much as I love my life with Luke, I don't enjoy living a lie. I don't want to continue this charade forever. My words tense as I proceed carefully. "Maybe we don't need to this May, but at some point, it might make sense." My words drop off as I don't even know what I'm saying. I should be happy, but a lot of our relationship—as good as it is—has been confusing.

He must have sensed my apprehension, as he takes the reins from me and gently pulls Buttercup to a halt. "Why are we stopping?" I turn to him, as tension grows.

"I can see that worry line above your brow, and there's no need for it." He wipes a stray hair that had blown in front of my face back behind my ear, and breathes out, "I love you, Noelle."

"I love you too." My words are weaker than I had planned. The air between us is thicker than normal, and my thoughts waver, as I'm not quite sure what is happening.

"You know I talked to my mom this morning."

"Oh." My voice is so tiny, I can barely hear it. "I still get the vibe that she doesn't like me."

"She mentioned something about that." He shakes his head, dismissing my concern. "She said she's going to apologize for not being more welcoming. It was overwhelming to hear her say she's seen a change in me that she likes, and she credits you."

"Really?" I chuckle, remembering how I was so scared of his mom a few months ago.

"Another thing that happened is she offered to plan a church wedding and reception for the summer. At first, I rolled my eyes and was going to grumble at her to mind her own business, but then I thought why not?" His hands animate in excited gestures. "It's perfect. We get to tie up the loose ends of our situation without having to let anyone know our little secret. We get to celebrate with our families, and nobody gets hurt."

My heart jams against my rib cage and my eyes spring wide. "What are you saying?"

"I'm saying, I know we had humble beginnings, but you've been the love of my life—since I was fourteen. You've consumed my thoughts, and I've reserved this little spot in my heart just for you. It's only grown over the years. Now I pray every day I live up to the potential of the man you deserve. The thought of breaking up in May—or ever—feels like a knife piercing my chest. I don't ever want to lose you." His words remain even, but tears well in his eyes as he continues, "I know I'm a travel grump, and you're a morning grump. You can't find a phone charger to save your life, but I seemingly always have one for you. Neither one of us is perfect, and we're bound to have things that annoy each other. You already have my ring, and I already did the proposal thing, but this time I'm asking for real. Do you want to get married this su mmer?"

I don't even blink. I twist the gold band I've already worn so faithfully and lean forward, pressing a kiss on his lips with my breathless, "Yes."

The cow presses his nose between us, breaking our kiss, and I laugh, redirecting my attention to him. "I guess, he's ready to move. Where are we going?" I tease, already knowing the path we always take.

"You know, over the river and through the woods."

I lean back, resting my head on Luke's shoulder as he pulls back on the reins and Buttercup moves forward. He knows the way to carry our sleigh . . . to *our* house we go.

And it's so perfect.

Somewhere off in the distant skies, way beyond the mountains, bells ring, and a matchmaking chuckle echoes, Ho-Ho-Ho.

Epilogue

Spring arrived early to our beloved chateau on the hill, and all the snow melted into green valleys filled with wild mountain laurel and milkweed. I was anxious to open the shutters and air out the house, even if it meant storing my sleigh in the barn for a few months.

Seamus loves it, getting into all the spring foliage, even the nasty smelling stuff like wormwood. It's a treasure to take Buttercup with him each morning, and I can't help but marvel that living out here in the mountains is my life.

If you would have told me a year ago, I'd be living my dream in the country with my horse and fluffy cow, and the man of my dreams, I'd never have believed it.

Today is Luke's college graduation, and the ceremony went off as expected with long speeches and an impressive roll call of graduating names. Luke's dad seemed to know most of the names, ad-libbing tidbits of information while Luke's mom didn't have much to say at all.

Now we hurry back to the house to do something Luke and I have been nervous about for a while—welcoming both our families to our home in celebration of Luke's graduation, and sort of a delayed holiday gathering since this last semester got away from us.

The first guest to arrive is Nate, alone.

I peek out the front door as he meanders up the dirt driveway, hands stuffed into his trousers and head lowered. When his eyes find mine, the corners of his mouth twitch into a satisfied grin and his arms open wide. My feet are moving before he gets to the porch, and I fly right into his hug. While I'm laughing gleefully, his expression is sober. "It's great to see you." I add another squeeze to my hug before we let go.

"Same." His expression slowly eases into a more relaxed smirk as he rocks back on his heels. "So, you and Luke. I must see this with my own eyes."

"Hard to believe, isn't it?" My lips pinch together as if to seal all the secrets Nate and I share.

"Maybe or maybe not." His bottom lip pushes out into a thinking stance. "I always knew Luke was a great guy or I wouldn't have arranged this whole thing. You were just the last to see it."

"So, you're taking credit for it, then?" I tease, a chuckle leaks from my mouth as I slowly start to pace back to the house to guide Nate inside.

He shrugs nonchalantly, and follows me inside, his gaze taking time to scan the room before Luke comes down the stairs. He's wearing another flannel shirt, as that seems to be his new wardrobe since we moved out here. It suits him more than the polo shirts, and I still blush when he throws a vest over the top of it. "Look who is here?" Luke calls out, striding over to pat Nate on the back. "Good to see you." He exaggeratedly looks behind him, teasing, "Where's your lady friend?"

"Ah, about that." Nate's gaze slides to me before his lips twitch down. "Noelle was right."

My heart twists, pumping harder as I'm worried. "Right about what?"

Nate shakes his head back and forth, before only offering a quick, "She wasn't who she said she was. When I got down there, she had all these excuses about why she couldn't ever see me, and it didn't take long for me to realize what was up."

"I was wondering why I never heard much from you." My heart drops, and all the months of low contact with Nate make sense. "Although, I had assumed you were just busy with her."

"Nah." He shakes his head again, as his gaze stays low. "I had a hard time finding work, and what I did get didn't pay the best, so I was working a lot, and I spent the savings I did have to get down there." When he raises his gaze to meet mine, we connect in a way we've always done. "And I was embarrassed. I knew I wanted to come home, but I also didn't have the money."

"Wait a second." I gesture forward, excitement budding in my chest. "You're moving back?"

"I want to, but I have to find a place and all."

Maybe I should drag Luke aside to have a private conversation first, but I'm too excited and I spring to the tips of my toes, "We have a room you can stay in!" After it's out, I slide my gaze to Luke. "Right?"

He's chuckling, easy going as ever, and gestures up in acknowledgement of all the rooms we have upstairs. "We do have a few we can spare."

"Nah." Nate shakes his head, his eyes hugging the ground now. "I couldn't take that from you after what I did to you both."

"We're not upset about what you did to us." I laugh as I reach out to squeeze Luke's forearm. "We definitely got over it, and it won't be forever. Just until you find work and your own place. We'd love to have you."

"Yeah, you're always welcome in our home." Luke doesn't wait a moment to allow silence and affirms. Then his gaze slides to me, a gleam sparks out of the corner of his eye, and he adds, "After all, we're all family."

My heart can't swell any fuller, as nothing can feel more perfect than that expression. My lips glide into a beaming smile. We have just a couple weeks left before Luke and I say our vows, and we will be family. I can't wait to say I do.

Thank you for reading, Let's Not and Sleigh We Did.

About J.P. Sterling

J.P. Sterling grew up watching old reruns of Lucille Ball and Mary Tyler Moore and fell in love with wholesome entertainment and slapstick comedy. She loves leaning into the over-the-top humor and full circle moments, especially if it means the underdog gets to shine.

Aside from writing, she's also a wife and homeschooling mom, a holistic dietitian, a former college professor and lover of all-things dark chocolate.

*No swears. Just kisses. No Blasphemies. *

Let's get social!

Hey you amazing reader! You are invited to join my private reader group for all-things clean books and friends. Enter the group here: https://www.facebook.com/groups/1500850764081965

Other places to follow me:

Instagram: https://www.instagram.com/stories/authorjpsterling/

Facebook: https://www.facebook.com/jpsterlingauthor/

Amazon: https://www.amazon.com/stores/author/B01N9TJXJN/about

Also by J.P. Sterling

***Christmas Shenanigans* (All Standalones)**

Mingle All the Way

Tis the Season to Get Married

Let's Not and Sleigh We Did

***The Coffee Loft Series* (All Standalones)**

Pardon My French Press

No More Mr. Chia Guy

***Sweet Hockey RomCom* (All Standalones)**

The Pucker-Up Pact

Shot Through the Heart

***A Modern Fairy Tale Series* (All Standalones)**

Royally Rugged

***Bosses and Billionaires Series* (All Standalones)**

Maid for my Billionaire Boss

Upcycling My Rig-Pig Boss

Kissed by My Billionaire Boss

Marooned with My Celebrity Boss

A Heart that Dances Series

Dancing on Broken Ankles

A Peek at Mingle All the Way

Jade O'lette

Schreeeeeech. Schreeeeeech.

Yanking the covers over my head so hard that I almost disjoint-
ed my shoulder, I held my breath and tuned into the I'm-clear-
ly-a-ghost-scratching sound outside my bedroom window. My
lungs screamed for oxygen, and I inhaled a deep breath of stale hot
air. Suddenly, the discounted price on my new rental house made
so much more sense. I had suspected something like this since it
was an older neighborhood. Not only a little old, but we're talking
colonial times. That's what the realtor called this house. A colonial.
All I saw was thirteen hundred dollars a month rent in a city where
nothing was under two thousand. I signed on the line so fast that
I practically left a smoke trail behind my pen.

This was my year of saving money, as I did whatever I could to
cut corners. If I did the mathing correctly, at the end of next year I
could pay off all my debt. All my student loans, plus the credit card
debt I had acquired after unexpectedly losing my middle-school

teaching job last spring. Having been locked into my old rental agreement and without a job, I drained every penny out of my savings, and then some. I did what I could to honor the contract, but even though I eventually found a job as a barista, I didn't make the same money as I had teaching. I fell further behind every month. Or at least until I found this budget rental at the exact time my previous rental contract expired.

Speaking of the discounted house, this was my first night in the house, and I'm not sure I signed up for a ghost. Unless he was like Casper, who transforms into a hot date for the dance. Christmas was around the corner, and I could use an escort for my work Christmas party.

"I'm beautiful, strong and brave," I whispered. It sounded dumb, but I had listened to this podcast where the dude said to repeat what you want to be. I'd been doing it for almost a year now, and bad things kept happening. It clearly wasn't working, but I was terrified of stopping. *What if it got worse?* "Oh, and rich," I added.

Schreeeeeech.

"I heard you!" I forced a brave voice as I peeled back my blanket, peeking out. "I know you're here, but I'm trying to sleep. You can cut it out now."

Schreeeeeech.

Tapping my finger to my chin, I mused. He's clearly a male ghost because he's pretending not to hear me.

Maybe I'll have a closer look.

I eased one foot off the bed, softly hitting the bare wood floor, and gently shifted my weight onto that leg, careful to not make a peep. Not sure why I was worried about disturbing mister-clamorous-hot-invisible dude when he obviously wasn't worried about *his* noise level.

Casing the four hundred square foot studio apartment, which was my part of the house, for a weapon, I settled on the broom stowed in the closet. Now to make my legs carry me across the room. I eased one foot before the other, tiptoeing across the squeaky wood floor. I opened the closet door, and my gaze unexpectedly landed on a pair of over-sized, glow-in-the-dark swimming goggles.

You never know . . .

Without a second thought, I tugged the goggles over my head, not taking the time to smooth out where the headband created a huge bubble of long dark hair above my head. I grabbed the broom, and a flashlight from the shelf, and Nancy Drew'd my way over to the window. I paused for a beat, swallowed the lump in my throat, and slowly exhaled. Breathing was so nice. Then I gradually peeled back the curtain . . .

Schreeeeeech.

"Ahh!" I jolted, my feet cementing to the floor in fright. My heart motored away, and even though I wasn't in danger, the moment's intensity left me lightheaded.

The neighbor's titanic tree branch dangled like creepy, giant fingers trying to claw into my room!

I breathed out a heavy release as the twiggy branch scraped against the metal siding until it thumbed off the side of the house.

A stupid branch! I held my chest, waiting for my heartbeat to slow.

A light switched on in the upstairs room in the house across the alley. Before I had time to think, a man stepped out on the upstairs veranda. He wore red flannel pajama pants and a white T-shirt. His hair was dark, with the perfect wave at the tips where it was slightly overgrown past his ears.

He was hot.

Somewhere in the universe, a calendar was missing their Mr. December.

My jaw fell. I could see him, but did that mean he could see me? I was standing here in my Christmas jammies and swimming goggles . . . I panicked and jerked the curtain closed. With a cringed expression on my face, I motored back to bed, yanking the covers tight around me, and rolled over on my side.

Now that I knew a ghost wasn't ready to wrap his fingers around my neck, I was finally ready to sleep.

Did Mr. December see me?

Nah, I'm sure he didn't.

The goggles. I forgotten I had them on, and they pinched the back of my neck. I started to yank them off, but my hair pulled with the elastic band. Wincing, I sucked in a hard breath. Get a grip, girl. I grabbed the front of googles and gave them an impatient tug over the back of my head. Now, I could finally rest. Squeezing my eyes shut, I tried not to think about the hunk across the alley, or how ridiculous I must have looked to him, no sir.

Schreeeeeech.

Already on Amazon and FREE in kindle unlimited. https://w ww.amazon.com/dp/B0CJCBNK6V

www.ingramcontent.com/pod-product-compliance
Lightning Source LLC
Chambersburg PA
CBHW061530310726
48972CB00008B/2388